CANNED
AND
CRUSHED

Bibi
Belford

New York

Sky Pony Press books may be purchased in bulk at special discounts for sales promotion, corporate gifts, fund-raising, or educational purposes. Special editions can also be created to specifications. For details, contact the Special Sales Department, Sky Pony Press, 307 West 36th Street, 11th Floor, New York, NY 10018 or info@skyhorsepublishing.com.

Sky Pony® is a registered trademark of Skyhorse Publishing, Inc.®, a Delaware corporation.

Visit our website at www.skyponypress.com.

10 9 8 7 6 5 4 3 2 1

Library of Congress Cataloging-in-Publication Data

Belford, Bibi.
  Canned and crushed / Bibi Belford.
    pages cm
  Summary: When his father, who is in the United States illegally, becomes injured and unemployed, eleven-year-old Sandro is determined to help his parents raise money for his little sister's heart surgery by collecting scrap metal to recycle for cash.
  ISBN 978-1-63220-435-6 (hc : alk. paper)
  [1. Illegal aliens—Fiction. 2. Unemployed—Ficiton. 3. Recycling (Waste)—Fiction. 4. Moneymaking projects—Fiction. 5. Racism—Fiction. 6. Mexican Americans—Fiction.] I. Title.
  PZ7.1.B45Can 2015
  [Fic]—dc23
                              2014039060

Ebook ISBN: 978-1-63220-833-0

Cover design by Georgia Morrissey
Cover photograph credit Thinkstock

Printed in the United States of America

This book is dedicated to the students of District 131 who have enriched my life and taught me more than I ever taught them; and to my colleagues who work hard to ignite a passion for reading every day.

CHAPTER 1

Explain Yourself

So, you notice I'm standing in the hall. Yes, I'm in trouble. You probably want to know why. Thirty seconds ago I told Miss Hamilton, my teacher with six toes on her right foot, that my dad's job was helping dead animals. She told me to go to the hall and be ready to explain myself. But how should I start to explain myself—I mean, in your opinion? How would *you* explain *yourself*?

I'm four feet, two-and-a-half inches tall. Shorter than most of the boys in my class but taller than at least five girls, so at least there's that. I'm eleven years and two weeks old. I had my birthday on the first day of school, which stinks. Anybody with an early September birthday really gets a raw deal.

I mean, Cheese Whiz, the birthday policy isn't even up and running by the first day of school. And how do you know which kids might be cool enough to invite to your birthday party? I only started at Lincoln Elementary last year in the spring when we moved across town, so it's tough to judge who's cool and who isn't.

Of course, by the second week of school, things are sorted out. Then those lucky birthday buzzards get to wear a crown and the whole class sings to them. Maybe they even get a birthday pencil. And if I did get to have a party, which I never do, by then I'd know exactly who to leave off the invite list. For starters, someone whose initials are A. K.

Not that my birthday is a big deal. I'm not Abiola Kahn for crying out loud. In third grade, Abiola's parents brought pizza and goodie bags to school to celebrate their "princess." There were little flower erasers for the girls and soccer ball erasers for the boys. Overboard, I say. Of course, if you want to make friends and win enemies, pizza and goodie bags are a start. But I'm off track here—let's get back to explaining about myself.

I'm supposed to be in fifth grade. I know what you're thinking. And no, I didn't flunk. When I was five I lived in Mexico, and the school in my town didn't have a kindergarten. So when I registered here, instead of putting me in first grade where I belonged, they stuck me in kindergarten. And look how well it worked. I'm smart and bilingual and the oldest of all the fourth graders in my class.

My hair is jet black. I got that color name from a label on one of my little sister's crayons. Jet Black. It sounds cool. Of course, I've never seen a black jet, have you? I remember the jet we took here from Mexico— purple with an orange sun on the side. Maybe fighter jets are jet black.

So here I am standing in the hallway. I'm not sure why I need to explain myself to Miss Hamilton. She can plainly see I'm four feet, two-and-a-half inches tall and good-looking with my jet black hair that is past my jet black eyebrows because I need a haircut.

Maybe I should start by explaining the things she can't see. Like how someday I want to be a professional soccer player. And also an inventor. I'm always thinking of better ways to make stuff.

Take, for example, a can of soda. Wouldn't it be great to have a fizz meter on it? At a party, when no parents are watching, you could turn it up and shoot soda spray up into the air or drink it so fast that your burps are louder than drag racers. And in the lunch- room at school, you could calibrate it to shoot discreetly at certain annoying girls sitting across from you at the lunch table.

Uh-oh. Here comes Miss Hamilton now. Watch and learn, compadres.

"Sandro?"

"Yes?"

"Are you ready to explain yourself?"

Now here's something that really bugs me about teachers and grown-ups in general. They ask you a question, but before you can answer the first question, they become a pitching machine and start firing questions at you—or worse, they answer for you.

"Sandro, do you make these stories up for attention? To get a laugh? Do you think you're funny?"

Of course, I'm not going to correct a teacher when she's on a roll, but that last comment was erroneous. Now that's an impressive word, isn't it? As you can see, I'm working on my vocabulary. I could just say false, but erroneous made you sit up and take notice, didn't it? Yah. I thought so.

Anyway, the whole class thought my answer was hysterical even though I wasn't trying to be funny. Abiola practically fell out of her perfect little desk, laughing uproariously, her long braid waving frantically. I think that's what got to Miss Hamilton. Maybe Miss Hamilton doesn't have a sense of humor. It's a little early in the school year to tell.

Here's what I've learned in my four years of elementary school experience so far. Squeeze your eyebrows together. Keep your lips tightly closed, and nod your head like you suddenly see things from the teacher's perspective. Miss Hamilton's shoulders shifted down when I did my little trick, and she moved her arms from her hips to crisscrossing her stomach. That's another good sign, by the way.

"Okay, Sandro. Tell me the truth. In *Charlotte's Web*, Fern's father makes a living by farming. How does your father make a living?"

I can see through the window in the door that the class is starting to lose it while we're out in the hall. My friend Miguel shot a three pointer with his crumpled paper wad, Jazzy made a fish face at me in the window of the door, and Rafe is catapulting pencils off his desk. I wonder what Lorenzo is doing over by the sink. I'm thinking fast. How should I answer this?

For one thing, why is a person's job described as "a living"? Living is breathing with your heart pumping. Is a person without a job dying?

Are these questions violations of some privacy law? Do I need a lawyer? Is this a courtroom? Raise your hand and tell the truth. The whole truth and nothing but the truth, so help you God.

Okay, I might be overreacting. I mean, this is only mildly annoying, except I do want to stick up for my dad. It's the principle of the thing. And speaking of principles, I really don't want to be sent to the principal for a second time in two weeks. Miss Hamilton didn't actually say the "whole truth," did she? Maybe a partial truth will do. Or maybe you would call it a little white lie. This truth thing can get pretty complicated.

Promise you won't go blabbing? Then I will tell you the "whole truth." My dad is officially laid off from his official job. He fell off a scaffold while he was putting shingles on a roof. He doesn't have a legal permit to work in the US so he can't get workmen's compensation or unemployment. He was working for a guy who knew my Uncle Pablo. You know how that goes.

I see your mind turning. Undocumented worker, you're thinking. Illegal. Well, nothing is as it appears on the surface. Remember that. Always go deeper. The tiny little iceberg triangle you see above the surface is a small portion of the giant mountain of ice underneath, big enough to sink the *Titanic*.

My dad has an engineering degree from the best technical institute in Mexico City. He has the same brilliant inventor ideas as me. But here's the thing— my dad comes from the ancient Zapotec people. The noblest Mexican Indians. Do you know anything about family heritage? Well, if you do, you know that people can get very proud about their family heritage. Being the best provider for his family is in my dad's blood. It's in my blood, too.

Since an engineer in Mexico gets paid two-thirds less than one in the US, my dad found an American company to sponsor him after he got his degree, but at the last minute, the job fell through. Did he give up? Nope. He was packed and ready to go, so he just risked everything and came here hoping the company would change its mind after meeting him in person. Sounds like a good idea, doesn't it?

Wrong-o. He should have waited and applied for a worker's permit. Now that he's "undocumented," everything is complicated. I try to ask questions to understand it better, but I don't. It's been five years, and now Dad says he can't compete with the brand new engineers and their technical knowledge. He says he needs to go back to school. But since me and Girasol and my mom came here to live with him four years ago, all he does is work. And guess what? He makes more money pounding nails in the US than engineers make in Mexico.

Now my dad is hurt, so my mom, who is still working on her English, got a cleaning job to pay the bills. Parents still need to feed their kids and take them to the doctor when they're sick. My dad can't lift heavy stuff, and he rubs his back and grunts when he stands up. But does he lie around and feel sorry for himself? Nope. Remember, his ancestors are the Zapotecs—the smartest, proudest Mexicans that ever lived. I want to be just like my dad.

He works two jobs now, but they're not real jobs. For one job, he picks up roadkill for the Department of Streets and Sanitation and gets paid by the carcass. Gross, huh? For the second job, he collects scrap metal to recycle for cash—things like rusty old bikes and pipes—with yours truly doing a lot of the lifting. Now what would you tell your nosy teacher about how your dad "makes a living"? Here's what I decide to do.

"My dad is unemployed."

"Thank you, Sandro. There's no shame in being unemployed. He'll find a job soon, I'm sure. Aren't you sorry you caused such a scene? Now let's turn over a new leaf, shall we?"

No, actually, I'm not sorry. I'm never sorry. Would the Avengers be sorry? Would my Zapotec dad be sorry? No way, José.

The "shall we" request reminds me of my visit to the principal on the first day of school. And if you're not too bored, I should probably tell you about it now, while I'm divulging all this information. On our first day, we took a tour of the grand old school, most likely to kill time while Miss Hamilton was memorizing our names. I mean, seriously, what do most of us care about at school? Making sure we know how to get to the playground, gym, and bathroom, not always in that order.

Anyway, our class climbed the flight of stairs from our second floor domain to the third floor where the fifth graders rule. They even have their own computer lab up there, so they don't have to associate with the rest of us. Last year we never went up to the third floor. I guess we were too young to be aware of the dangers. I mean, there is just that one railing, and it's a long way down. I think by the time we got up there we heard one thousand "shall we's."

"Let's be quiet in the hallway, shall we? Let's take a peek in the library, shall we? Let's show the first graders our best manners, shall we?"

So at the top of the stairs, of course, we knew a "shall we" was coming.

"Let's keep our hands on this side of the railing, shall we?"

And I snapped. Just like that. I mean, what was the good of being higher up in the sky than I had ever been except for that one airplane ride? So I leaned over that railing and let fly the biggest wad of spit I could muster on short notice. And from way down on the first floor, you could actually hear a splat, which was exactly what I was hoping for.

But then a face looked up from the first floor, and the next thing I knew I wasn't on the tour anymore. Instead, I'm in Principal Smalley's office, and his face looks even madder than it did from way down on the first floor. And while I'm supposed to be thinking about my actions, I'm really thinking about Principal Smalley and wondering if he was ever a kid who let fly a wad of spit. So anyway, that's how fourth grade is going for me. Day One—office visit. Week Two—hall visit.

I follow Miss Hamilton back into the classroom. She doesn't notice the kids scurrying into place or the pencils poking down from the ceiling. I sit, and my backside feels wet. I immediately know what Lorenzo was doing at the sink. ARGH! He better not linger around after school. I stare at my open copy of *Charlotte's Web*, but all I see is my dad. The crinkles around his eyes. The rock-like muscles of his arms. The tree smell on his cheeks after he shaves. And how he laughs when Girasol and I tackle him and tickle.

Fern's dad kills animals for a living because he's a farmer, and no one thinks that's gross? My dad just picks them up off the street and puts them in a landfill where they can decay gracefully. Now I'm asking you, what do you think? Which one is more humane?

CHAPTER 2

Nothing Is As It Appears

Miguel and I are sucking on giant jawbreakers that Abiola passed out while we toss an old tennis ball against the school's brick wall. We're waiting for our sisters, who come out the same door even though Girasol is in kindergarten and Marta is in first grade. Miguel, Marta, and Girasol still speak Spanish better than English, so after school I speak Spanish, too. But since I'm not sure about your home language, I'm just going to translate everything for you as we go along.

"Are you going to make a picture for the contest?" Miguel's jawbreaker makes it hard to understand him.

"I think so. You?" I take out my jawbreaker to see if Abiola lied about it changing colors. She always brings stuff to give away to the class as if that will make people like her. I want to tell her you can't buy friends, but why ruin my supply of free stuff?

Miguel misses catching the ball and chases it down. "For two hundred dollars? For sure."

"Cheese Whiz! That's what I was thinking."

In art class today, Mrs. Abernathy advertised a contest. The school district is going to put the twelve best students' drawings into a calendar. Every page will have coupons for local businesses, like Dynamo Donuts and Kleen Cleaners. Even after the school pays the twelve winners two hundred dollars each, they hope to make a lot of money selling the calendars to the community.

I am thinking about which month I want to draw. It seems to me most kids might go for October and December, seeing as how pumpkins and Christmas trees are easy to draw, so I bet those months will get a lot of competition.

I already know what I'm going to buy with the two hundred dollars once I win. Oh yah. The most amazing, awesome, super-fantastic bike. Shock absorbers on the T-bone. Flames on the frame. Shimano 21-Speed Twist Shifters. I'm not going to be getting that kind of present from my parents anytime soon. But with two hundred dollars? No problem. "You can wrap it up," I'll tell the store man.

"What month are you going to draw?" I ask Miguel.

"What month are *you* going to draw?" he asks me back.

"I dunno."

"Me too."

But the way he says it makes me think he does know, but he's not going to tell me, which is fine by me. I have to help Miguel with lots of stuff, but Miguel is pretty good at drawing. Not as good as me, though, so if we pick the same month and I win the money—well, he might feel pretty low.

"Today we practice soccer before the game, yes?"

"I can't. I have to help my dad. It's Wednesday."

Miguel scowls. "You work always. This game is big."

"I'll hurry." Miguel just wants to be sure I'm there to score the goals for our team. But that will depend on my dad's luck with the recycling and if he finds any treasures—tesoros, he calls them. You would call them trash. Not my dad. Every scrap of metal equals money for us.

We see our sisters coming out of the doors. Marta and Girasol love each other. Little kids are weird that way. They hug and hold hands and sing and chant stuff. Miguel and I follow them down the sidewalk. It's like being with two parrots that don't stop yapping.

Miguel and Marta just arrived from Mexico last year. Have you ever been to Mexico? Let me tell you about it. The border towns are for tourists. By border towns, I mean the towns that border California and Texas. They have lots of junk shops with lots of paraphernalia. Now don't freak out because I used a big word. You're smart, aren't you? Remember, I'm trying to work on my vocabulary to sound smart. That big word means stuff. Stuff that tourists buy. T-shirts, key chains, hats, and stuffed iguanas. Now that's some interesting roadkill, huh?

But when you go farther into Mexico, you see green mountains and blue oceans sometimes running right into each other. Sure, there are a lot of people there who don't have as much as we do, but a kid has a lot to do in Mexico, especially where we lived in the Central Valley, near the city of Oaxaca. Just so you know, it's pronounced Wa-Ha-Ka. It's hot and humid and the skies turn foggy to sunny, with muddy streets in the rainy summer season. Like I said, there's lots to do. Forests to wander, waterfalls to jump, rivers to swim, horses to ride, stones to throw, soccer balls to kick, and rattlesnakes to shoot.

Aha. You were starting to get bored with all this description, weren't you? But stories need settings. You know that. So, you're interested in the rattlesnake story?

Remember, I was just a little grasshopper when we left Mexico. I was at my abuelo's ranch, and we went to throw some hay into the corral. The corral fences in Mexico are just wires strung between branches then stuck into the ground—cheap but effective. Horses and cows scrounge around and nibble on the sagebrush, but it's not enough. You know what they say: hay is for horses.

Well, we were getting close to the fence and one of the horses made a loud sound, a sort of screaming neigh. I wish you could hear me do it. It would send shivers up your spine. We stopped dead in our tracks. Not really dead. That's what the horse was trying to tell us. Stop or you'll be dead.

There on the path, curled up like a piece of gray rope, a rattlesnake lifted its head and hissed. You know those photos you see on Google images of rattlesnakes? If you don't know, go look one up. I'll wait. So you got it in your mind? Well, they're right on target. They make this sound with their tail—imagine little rocks shaking around in an empty soda can.

Abuelo said, "Sandro, stay put, don't move"—in Spanish, of course. Miss Hamilton would have said, "Let's not move, shall we?" Abuelo's voice made me freeze even though I wanted to run. And stay put I did with that snake just about as far away as the length of a bat—a baseball bat, not the one that flies.

Now if you want to be a good reader, you have to get a well-defined picture in your mind. There's me, there's the snake hissing and shaking, and there's the horse screaming, in that order. I knew grandpa was behind me, so you can put him in the picture even though I couldn't see him. All of a sudden the loudest sound I've ever heard jammed into my ears. Actually, the sound reverberated in all my joints. Uh-oh. Big word alert. Reverberated means bounced back and forth.

Seems that when you're going to shoot a gun, you should give a warning. In golf the players yell, "Fore." In baseball they yell, "Play ball." In racing they shout, "Get ready, get set," and then they shoot the gun. But a gunshot with no warning made me jump so high I thought Abuelo blew us both to kingdom come. I never even knew Abuelo carried a gun in his belt. That rattlesnake didn't know it either. It flopped right down to the ground, sorry it ever woke up that morning to say, "Make my day."

So lots of times when I'm with Miguel my mind wanders off to Mexico, and thinking about Mexico makes me think about Abuelo. And thinking about Abuelo always brings up that memory of that rattlesnake. And right this minute while I'm telling you all this background info, Girasol trips over nothing and lands flat on her face with Marta so close behind that she falls over my sister.

"Girasol!" I shout and rush to her. I pull on her backpack to help her up.

She's crying, and Marta is hollering and holding her stomach. "Ow, ow, ow!"

Girasol has a gash on her chin and scrapes on both hands and knees. She's blubbering now, and the tears and nose stuff and blood is sort of mixing together as she rubs her chin. Yah. Gross.

"Doe-doe," she blubbers. That's how she says my name, "Doe-doe." She's called me that ever since she learned to talk.

"Stop, stop. Here," I say and pull my T-shirt off to clean her up. I'm no doctor, but she looks okay, just dinged up a little. The blood on her chin is starting to coagulate. I know, another big word. But you seem intelligent, so I don't want to dummy it down for you. Work with me here. Co as in cooperate—it means together. So blood coming together, or stopping bleeding, is coagulate. See how smart you're getting? Stick with me—we're going places!

That's when I think I see the rattlesnake I was just telling you about. The scaly brown face with the puppet grin. Those beady eyes—and it's coming out of Girasol's backpack. I blink and shake my head.

Then Miguel says, "Qué es eso?"

And sure enough, I'm not losing my mind. I see now it's definitely not a rattlesnake. Its toes are climbing over the edge of the backpack. And it's attached to a shell. And then I recognize it. The school mascot, Franklin the turtle.

"Girasol, what are you doing with Franklin?" I ask, pulling Franklin out and holding him gently.

Girasol is still blubbering, so it's hard to understand her. "I want him. He's mine. Give him back."

"No, Girasol. You can't just take the turtle from school."

I hold the turtle higher since she's jumping and reaching while blubbering and screaming.

"Why? Why do you want it?" I ask her.

"For vanilla. Mrs. Diaz said he gives vanilla. I want vanilla."

Yes, you heard right. And I agree with you. What connection do turtles have with vanilla? But remember, nothing is as it appears. And that is when I decide I should start writing these things down so people will believe me when I tell them about my life.

•

Miguel figures it all out as we finish the walk home, taking turns giving Franklin the fright of his life. I know I said this before, but always remember, nothing is as it appears on the surface.

Girasol met Franklin on the school tour, just the same way we all met Franklin. Every year, the teachers explain that wild animals are not to be played with.

"Play with my own. Leave wild ones alone." That's the catchy little poem they teach kids to help them remember about wild animals. The last thing the teachers tell kids about Franklin is, "Franklin looks friendly, but he's a turtle, and turtles may give you salmonella, so don't touch Franklin."

If you were learning English for the first time, do you think you would know about salmonella? But if you went to The Banana Split every day in the summer and the girl behind the counter asked if you wanted chocolate or vanilla, do you think you would know about vanilla?

So you can see how Girasol got a little mixed up. Try it. Say salmonella then vanilla. Thing is, salmonella is a bacteria that makes you sick, and vanilla is the only flavor ice cream Girasol ever eats. Now why don't you try explaining that to Girasol?

CHAPTER 3
Look Below the Surface

We turn onto our street, and Miguel hands me his grammar homework. He finishes it in class so I can look it over in the evenings. I don't think that's cheating, do you? I just check it, and if it's wrong, he fixes it. We have grammar homework every night this year, and in my opinion, that's over-kill. Last year, in third grade, we only had grammar homework once a week. But Miguel is getting better with English this year, so maybe practice does make perfect.

"Don't be late for soccer," he says.

"I'll hurry," I say for the second time.

What's the first thing you do when you get home from school? Yep, me too. Just walking in the door makes me hungry. But first things first. I tell Girasol to be brave while I clean her up. I do my impressions of cartoon characters to make her laugh. If we ever meet, I'll show you, and you'll laugh, too. I get the rag super wet and sudsy the way my mom does, so Girasol only whimpers a little when I do her knees. Maybe I'll be an EMT comedian one day.

I rustle up some snacks and turn on the TV. Girasol curls up next to me and goes to sleep. I'm thinking about Franklin. Here's what I think. Franklin will die if I leave him in Girasol's backpack. And Franklin will die if my dad sees him. Remember one of my dad's jobs? Well, you should know that, he's paid by the carcass. Adiós, Franklin. I could put him in a box, but if he gets out my mom might die of fright. And even though Girasol stole Franklin, we all know yours truly will be blamed. I'm a dead man.

I could walk Franklin back to school right now. This is a bad idea for three reasons. First, my dad might come home and find me gone just when he's ready for an amazing haul. Second, it's too early for Mrs. Arona in the duplex next door to be home to watch Girasol, and she's too little to be left alone. And third, with my luck Principal Smalley would be up on the third floor spying on me sneaking around the first floor with Franklin.

Then I have a brainstorm. I grab the olla from under the counter. It's a big pot we use for tamales but not very often. I put a little dish of water in the pot. Girasol is still asleep, so I sneak outside and spoon some dirt into the pot, thinking Franklin might like it if some bugs just happened to be mixed in with the dirt. Then I throw in some handfuls of grass, introduce Franklin to his new home, and put the olla back under the counter, with the heavy lid on tight. No way can Franklin escape from my ingenious solution.

I hear my dad's truck. So that's good. I might make it back in time for soccer. I really hate missing soccer practice. Once inside, my dad thumps me on the back. "How was school?" he asks. "Keep out of trouble?"

"Yep," I say. "How's treasure hunting?"

"Good. Maybe ten."

That's not good for me getting to soccer, but it is good for money. Ten means ten places that might still have scrap metal. If no one beats us there. Because of my dad's back, he has to wait for me to help him lift the stuff into the truck. He used to wait for my Uncle Pablo, but by the time his work ended, everything was picked clean. I feel bad leaving when Girasol is asleep, but Mrs. Arona is home now to keep an eye on her. So we head out.

We stop a few blocks away, where we find an old iron metal bed. We get ready to lift the headboard into the back of the truck, and I stick my head through the bars of the bed and say, "Let me out. Let me out," pretending I'm in jail. I crack myself up.

My dad gives me a quick smile, but he doesn't laugh. I suddenly realize maybe he thinks I don't like working with him. As if working with him is the same as being in jail. I lay the headboard down, and instead of clowning around, I bust my butt muscling stuff into the truck. Three more stops for more metal stuff—a weight bench and weights, car parts at my dad's friend's garage, and some gutters. We pass on the refrigerator.

"Next year, when you grow up," my dad says.

I could probably lift it now, but I hate to show off. We drive past places five and six because nothing is left. Somebody beat us to it. Less work for me, but it makes my dad grumble under his breath. By the time we finish and head to the dealer, the truck is pretty full, including the cans my dad collected during the week. We pull into Crusher, Inc. with thirty minutes until soccer and three trucks in front of us.

If you've never been to a scrap metal yard, you've never lived. Piles of dead twisted metal carcasses surround the drive like an iron jungle. A huge, hungry crane with a giant magnet swoops around plucking pieces of metal as if picking flowers. The oily smell sort of burns your nose, and even if you try to stay clean, the dirt just jumps on you.

When it's our turn, we drive up onto a giant flat metal bed that's really a scale. It's the same drill every time. Get out. Grab the cans. Go wait in a little room. Give the cans to the lady. The lady behind the desk writes down the price for the cans and prints off the truck's weight. Some days we have a radiator or an air conditioner in the back of the truck. Those are in a different price category. Those are good treasures. Today, it's just regular stuff. My dad signs for it.

We get back in the truck and drive off the scale and down whichever path a worker wave us to. On a lucky day, the workers help us unload, throwing the heavy metal stuff onto the metal mountains as if they're flicking feathers. But today is unlucky. Somehow, I knew it would be. The workers are helping other luckier dads, so we grunt and sweat and pull the stuff out and lay it beside the big mountains.

Then we drive the truck back onto the scale and go back in the little room. The lady weighs the empty truck, and then she does subtraction. Here's the problem for you: The full truck weighed 6,597 pounds and the empty truck weighs 6,520 pounds. What's the difference? Well that number is the pounds of metal we get paid for, and every pound is worth fifty cents. While you figure that out, I'll tell you a story.

One time when we were waiting in the little room, a couple of boys came to the office with two bikes. The lady didn't even make them weigh the bikes. She gave them $8.75. They threw the bikes on the mountain, and later, when we drove down the street to go home, I saw those two boys sitting on the curb eating McDonald's hamburgers.

I felt sad for a minute, thinking they were so hungry that they traded their bikes for hamburgers. Then I wondered if they stole the bikes, and I felt sad for the real owners, too. My dad touched my arm and pointed behind the boys. Guess what I saw? Yep. The bikes. So it goes to show you, always look below the surface. Also, before you feel sorry for somebody, make sure they are not a cheater.

Today, me and my dad get $23.10 for the cans in cash and a check from the lady for $38.50. Is that the answer you got? See, I knew you were smart. She gives me a peppermint like that will sweeten up the place, and we head home.

I don't bother putting on my shin guards or shoes because once the game has started, the refs won't let me in late. I'm glad my dad doesn't say anything stupid like, "It's just a game, Sandro." He's a big soccer fan. It's not his fault half the games are on the same day people put their garbage out for the next day's pickup. I'm disappointed, of course, but I stay cool so my dad doesn't notice.

The only thing is, the team needs me. We're unde-feated and have five more games in the regular season. If we win at least three, we go to the playoffs. And if we win the playoffs, we go to the championship. Oh yah. I hope the team wins today, but I also hope they don't start somebody else and leave me on the bench for the next game. And you know, I live and breathe soccer. It will kill me if that happens. Every day at recess, we kick the ball around. Just us guys. Soccer is a game for guys, don't you think? No offense, but I think girls should stick to jump rope and gymnastics—stuff they can do well.

At home I smell dinner, so that's good, cuz I'm hungry and dirty and have homework.

"Sandro, what happened to Girasol?" my mom asks.

I tell her, and she shakes her head.

"But how? Was she running? Did she trip over something?"

I think back. "No," I say. "She was walking and fell down, I guess."

"She has a fever. Maybe she got dizzy." And my mom shakes her head again. That worried shake, the way your mom probably does, too. Like shaking the eight ball until the answer comes into view and clears everything up.

I don't think too much about it because Girasol is five and just barely past a baby in my book. Babies fall all the time, don't they? I work on some homework and then eat dinner, or I should say devour dinner. It's a good thing moms love to cook, isn't it? I know some families don't eat together, but we do, and I'm glad.

My mind is bouncing around while I'm chewing.
Every once in a while I answer my mom's questions
about school, but mostly I bounce around in my head
between which month to draw for the contest and how
to get Franklin back to school. Here's my thinking:
November—I would have to draw people for Thanksgiving, and people are hard to draw. Franklin—leave him
outside on the step. No, it might be too cold. January—
it snows in January, and drawing white snow on white
paper doesn't sound too appealing. Franklin—I could
bring him back to school tomorrow in my backpack.
But what if he poops or pees while he's in there?

I'm starting to think about drawing February and
asking Miguel to return Franklin for me when we hear
a noise in the kitchen, and my mom yells out, "Girasol,
what are you doing in there?"

Did I mention that Girasol didn't eat with us
because she had a fever? I might have skipped telling
you that because I was preoccupied with eating. Anyway, Girasol doesn't answer, so we all go back to eating.
A big fork full of chicken is heading into my mouth
when I hear the noise again. It sounds like Girasol
is getting a plate out of the cupboard. It sounds like
Girasol is scraping a spoon across the bottom of a
metal bowl. It sounds like Girasol is washing a pan
with a scrub brush. It sounds like . . . and then I know
what it sounds like.

It sounds like Franklin is escaping from his temporary home in the olla. I shoot out of my seat. "I'll go see!" I yell.

"Sandro!" my mom shrieks, and I see the table reverberate, glasses wobbling.

Whoops, my bad. But I'm in the kitchen before anyone else and just in time to see our friend waddle out the other door. The cupboard door is open, and the lid of the olla is on the floor. How in the world? Franklin must be an escape artist. I should have duct-taped the lid on. Holy guacamole. What should I do now? Two choices. Clean up the floor? Or follow Franklin?

"Sandro!" I hear my mom's voice and know she is at the kitchen door. "What is this mess?"

"Sorry. For school. A project." Here's another little bit of advice. If you make a weird mess, always say it's for a school project. Parents love school projects.

I'm scooping up the dirt and rinsing out the pan when my mom says, "What project?"

I'm thinking fast now. "Oh, you know, making homes out of stuff." I know there's a word, a big word, that will impress her. We learned it last year. It's the word for the places animals live. *Habitat.* That's it. "I'm making a habitat."

Mothers love to help out, so I know my mom will totally bite on this, and sure enough, she goes back into the living room. "Papi, do you have something Sandro can use for his project?"

See? I knew it. But where exactly is my other project? The one with the beady eyes? I walk down the hall and into Girasol's bedroom just in time to see a tail disappear under her bed. I'm just about to reach under to grab it when I take a look at Girasol.

"Mom! Mom!" I yell. And not just a regular yell. A panic yell. The kind of yell moms run for. The kind of yell you would yell if you saw your sister with a bloody nose and red blotches all over her face.

CHAPTER 4

Worry about Yourself

I'm going to skip ahead a bit in the story. It turns out Girasol is sick. Not just the flu kind of sick. The serious kind of sick. It started with something called Kawasaki disease. And no, not Kawasaki like the motorcycle. Turns out, this disease is all about blood vessels that get swollen. Mostly little kids get it, and after a few weeks, with medicine, they get better. Once in a while, though, an important artery to the heart gets so swollen that the doctors have to make a detour around it or put in new parts.

For some strange reason, it makes me feel queasy when I think about it. I'm kind of nervous, and I don't like to talk about it. I worry about all the times I wasn't a good brother. Sometimes I forget all about Girasol being sick and start having a good time. Then *whamo*, I remember and feel guilty because I forgot.

Like now, for example. I'm at soccer practice. Miguel will be giving me a ride home because Girasol and Mom and Dad are going to another doctor. A blood specialist. I need to focus on that round black and white ball, but I keep spacing out. I don't want anybody to feel sorry for me because I have a sick sister. I would hate that.

We're having a scrimmage against a team from another level. It's a game that doesn't count, but we pretend it's a real game to prepare for the playoffs. Remember I told you about that? We're not undefeated anymore. I missed a couple of games and practices because of Girasol, and we lost both of them. I don't want to sound proud or anything, but I did score two goals in our last crucial game, so I'm partly responsible that we made it to the playoffs.

The line is moving. Our keeper just kicked the ball down the field. Noel, our center midfielder, has control. He's not my favorite person, and I'm not his. His dad is the assistant coach, so Noel always plays, but I don't think he's that great. I guess it's one of those unfair things you have to deal with in life. "Worry about yourself, Sandro," my dad always tells me.

Right now I have to worry I don't get called offside. That always happens when I don't watch. I'm flying now. I keep Noel in my peripheral vision, and he passes the ball, but not to me. To Charlie. Cheese Whiz. I'm open, and Charlie has two defenders covering him. This is what happens when you don't show up for practices. Now I'm covering the tall guy who is streaking downfield toward our goal. Sure enough, I was right. The ball is passed right to his feet. Oh man, he's really quick, but some fancy footwork and—hold on, I have to concentrate.

Okay, so I was able to get the ball away from rocket man and pass it back to our sweeper. Forget about center mid Black Hole Noel. Now Miguel has the ball, and I know he will pass it to me. So I'm dodging around keeping open. Red jerseys are running toward me. Red blurs. Red, red, red, and suddenly I see Girasol with her white cheeks and her blood sickness, and I freeze.

You know how they say your life can flash before your eyes? It does. It takes just a nanosecond for me to see my family getting poorer and poorer and Girasol getting sicker and sicker. I see my mom and me and Girasol going back to Mexico and living with my abuelos and my dad sending us money the way he used to. I see my mom getting sadder and sadder with no job and no money and no hope and me having to go back to third grade because I don't know how to read and write in Spanish.

"NO!" I scream.

Then, *blam*, I snap out of it and connect with the ball just before three red blurs crash into me. And from down on the ground, I hear my team screaming and the ref blowing the whistle. I shake myself off. The goal is good. And there's a penalty called for the flagrant foul one of those red blurs did to me.

I'm okay. But not okay enough to take the penalty kick, so the coach chooses guess who? Noel. Of course he misses, but we still win. Yeah! We win. Oh yah, I almost forgot, it's just a scrimmage, but still, we beat the next level up, so that's a good sign.

The coach gives us our pep talk and puts his hand on my shoulder. "Great goal. Hope you can make it to the playoff game in two weeks," he says.

"Yah, hope you can make it," Noel says with a really nasty smile.

"And I hope you can pass to the open player," Coach says to Noel without a smile in his voice.

So that makes me feel better. Maybe Black Hole Noel is on borrowed time. Before we leave, we all have to take five penalty shots, and if anyone misses we have to start over. Everyone knows it's because Noel missed the penalty shot, and I want to say, "Thanks, Black Hole," in a very sarcastic voice. But I keep my mouth shut. *Worry about yourself, Sandro*, I say in my head, since my dad isn't there to say it.

Miguel's mom drops me off at home, and I can see my parents aren't back yet. That's okay because I have two important things to do. I've decided to draw February for the calendar contest. No, not that mushy Valentine stuff. I'm going to draw a really cool model of a heart with the valves and everything. I got the idea from listening to my mom and dad talk about Girasol's heart. I checked out two books from the library. I want to make it like a cartoon with speech bubbles coming out of the parts of the heart. It's hard to explain, so you'll just have to wait to see it.

Franklin is the other important thing. Yes, I know. You thought because I skipped ahead in my story that Franklin was taken care of. Wrong-o. And yes, the whole school is on Franklin alert. I swore Miguel to secrecy. I don't even know if Franklin is alive. Girasol's bed is too heavy for me to move, and the two-inch slot that Franklin crawled through is too narrow for my arm. I tried to use a flashlight, but going in your sister's room with a flashlight is a little suspicious.

Besides, Girasol pretty much lives in her room now with Mom or Dad always checking on her or sitting by her. She even has a little TV on her dresser that some lady at my mom's cleaning job let her borrow. The kid part of me is jealous of the TV, but the growing-up part of me knows I should be happy Girasol has something fun to do while she's sick.

During the first week that Girasol was sick, I thought I heard some scratching noises coming from her room. I started throwing vegetables under the bed when no one was looking. A lettuce leaf here and there. A carrot once in a while. I hope Franklin is not picky. I know turtles eat bugs, but it doesn't seem like such a good idea to put bugs under the bed. Girasol hates bugs.

Tonight, I get the broom and unscrew the bottom from the handle. Then I get a hanger and duct tape. If you don't have duct tape at your house, you really need to invest in some. It costs around four dollars, but it's worth gold. You can fix your shoe, make a trap, hang stuff from your ceiling—just about anything—with duct tape. Once I saw a book at the book fair that told kids how to make duct tape underwear. All I'll say is don't try it unless you have the book in front of you. Ouch!

I stretch out the hanger so it looks like a hook and duct-tape it to the handle of the broom. I worry it's too sharp and that I might poke poor, unsuspecting Franklin's soft underbelly, so I duct-tape one of Girasol's little socks over the pointy end. It's a little wobbly, but if Franklin is still alive, it might poke him into action.

I head to Girasol's room. I always feel a little sick myself when I go into her room. At first I thought I could catch her disease, so I always stopped at the door. Finally my mom figured out why I did that and told me it isn't contagious.

Girasol was at the hospital for a week, so I stayed with Miguel. Then she came home. Then she was at a different hospital farther away for a week, and I missed school to stay with my mom in a motel. My dad didn't want to lose a week of work, and my mom was scared she didn't speak enough English to survive on her own, so I had to go along. That hospital did tests and found out the disease had caused complications with a vessel or a valve in Girasol's heart.

I thought it would be cool to miss school and stay in a motel, but the TV only got four channels, and between the boring hospital and the boring motel room, even Miss Hamilton looked good when I got back. I'm still not caught up with all the work I missed, which reminds me of one more important thing I have to do.

I'm lying flat on my stomach, the flashlight beside me and shining under the bed. I'm pretty sure I see a blob that could be Franklin. I push the broom under the bed and move it toward the blob. The hook on the turtle rescue wand is sideways so I can gently scoop Franklin out from under the bed. I think it's working. The blob is getting closer. He's not crawling away so maybe he's asleep or sick or . . . oh dear.

What will I do if Franklin died under the bed? I'll have to cover up the murder and live with my guilt for the rest of my life. All those little kids wondering what happened to their beloved mascot, Franklin, thinking he is on the run enjoying his freedom, when really he's in turtle heaven.

And while I'm thinking and scooping, the blob is getting closer until it is right in front of me, and I see fur. What is your first thought? Mine, too. Decay and decomposition. Things in the back of the fridge get furry before my mom throws them out, so I'm thinking, *Poor Franklin.*

I'm deciding if I need to go put gloves on before I touch the corpse when I hear a noise. It's coming from the other side of the bed. I slide over and roll the flashlight along with me. And there he is. The con artist. Trying to switch identities with the furry blob. His eyes shine, and he looks very satisfied with himself. I grab the furry blob and pull with all my strength. Girasol's slipper pops out. And right then I hear the back door slam open. Uh-oh! I push the broom handle under the bed and skedaddle out of the bedroom.

Girasol is the color of a bone. Her eyes are closed. I don't understand how just one month ago she was happy and playing and annoying me every day and now she is a fragile egg. Dad lays her down on the couch.

"How was the game?"

"Good. How was the doctor?"

My dad looks at my mom. He doesn't say anything. Not a good sign. My mom ruffles my hair. Another bad sign. Why do moms do that anyway? My mom runs her finger under her eye, then goes into the kitchen.

My dad and I are just sort of standing there. It's awkward. I can't think of anything to say. Should I tell him about the goal I scored? About Noel missing the penalty shot? It all seems stupid compared to my sister looking so sick and my mom looking so sad. There's a word I'm thinking of that means little and unimportant. Trivial. That's the word. I wonder what's the opposite of trivial. Cuz that's what Girasol is to me.

"Mijo, you want to eat?" Moms know everything, don't they? I'm starving. She puts tortillas and meat and beans on the table, and we eat. That is, my dad and I eat. I guess no matter what, guys can always eat.

"Sandro, we have something to tell you." My dad is using his serious voice. Like he did when I was in third grade, and I accidentally pushed Abiola off the slide during recess because she claimed I cut in front of her. And like he did when I accidentally put a bag of M&Ms into my pocket without paying for them.

I feel like I'm in the hall again waiting to explain myself. Or sitting in Mr. Smalley's office.

"Girasol needs an operation. It costs a lot of money here, but in Mexico it is cheaper."

No, no, no. My head is exploding. My worst nightmare is coming true. Did I make it come true by imagining it? One of the Avengers says, "Visualize it, and it will be."

I love Mexico, but I want to live here. I'm about to become a soccer sensation. I'm going to buy a fantastic new bike. I've discovered Franklin is alive. I'm going to be a famous inventor. My dad is still talking, but I haven't heard a word he's said.

"So you will have to be responsible. Maybe in the summer you can go, too."

Here's the thing about not listening. You miss information. Important information. What did he say? Responsible for what? Go where? Sometimes it just works best if you're honest.

"Dad, I, uh, got hit pretty hard in soccer today, and I think my ear is still a little swollen. Could you say that again?"

"Sandro." My dad starts to get mad.

"Papi, he has a lot to think about. He's only a boy."

Thank goodness for moms. They always come to your rescue. So my dad explains all over again. This time I listen. It ends up, I'm not going to Mexico. Just my mom and Girasol. They're going to stay with my abuelos while they are waiting for the surgery and then after the surgery while Girasol is recovering. And I know she will recover. "Visualize it, and it will be."

So I have to be responsible. Go to school. Help my dad. Then maybe go to Mexico in the summer.

I should explain something here. My dad can't go to Mexico at all because he doesn't have a visa.

Not the credit card Visa, but something you have to have if you are a citizen of one country and want to live in another country.

My mom doesn't have to worry. She's a US citizen because she was born in San Diego and then moved to Mexico. And, technically, my dad shouldn't worry because he's married to my mom, which gives him the right to live here. But immigration doesn't know that because my dad's been a little negligent on the paperwork. He hates applications. And he's worried he might be fined, deported, or worse if immigration finds out he's been here all this time without a visa. He calls it red tape, but I've never seen any of that lying around the house—just piles of paper.

He always reads the news about immigration reform and says, "Someday, Sandro, they will make a way for us." His bright hopes and dreams that gave him the courage to take the risks to come here are getting duller. He used to read his engineering books after dinner while I did my homework. He used to look for new companies to sponsor him. Now he just works and falls off roofs.

I agree. It's all very confusing. Why do they make such complicated rules? Doesn't it seem unfair? My hardworking dad can't even go see his own parents in Oaxaca, but my mom, who hates to fly, can travel all over the world.

"So, Sandro, will you take care of Papi for me?" My mom ruffles my hair again and clears the table.

I nod. I hope we don't starve to death. I have that jumpy feeling again. Relieved and worried. Hopeful and scared. I want to ask if Girasol will be back to normal after the operation, but I know they don't tell me these things because I'm just a kid and they don't want to worry me. Just like I don't tell them Noel is a jerk, that Miss Hamilton hates me, and that Franklin is missing (well, technically, that he's under the bed).

And then, right before my eyes, standing at the door in her pink jeans and sparkly T-shirt, I see Girasol. And in her two hands, close to her heart, she has Franklin.

"Ayeeiii!" shouts my mom.

"Sandro!" shouts my dad.

"Look, Doe-Doe. It's Franklin," says Girasol as I rush over and take Franklin before she drops him.

After I explain how Franklin came to be visiting the Zapote house (without so much as a peep from Girasol, the original turtle stealer), my dad says, "When were you going to tell us about this? Not telling information is as bad as lying."

"I was just going to return him but then Girasol got sick and—"

My dad holds up his hand. "Tomorrow. And I want you to tell the principal how sorry we are. Is this understood, or do I need to help you?"

Girasol grabs Dad's arm. "No, Papi. Please. Please let him stay."

My dad doesn't say yes or no. Instead, he puts his thumb on the corner of one eye and his finger on the corner of the other, then pulls them together and walks away.

"Take care of Papi for me," Mom says again. "Girasol, go back to bed. We're leaving in the morning."

CHAPTER 5

Be the Better Man

I'm not proud of this next part of the story. And I won't blame you if you want to stop reading. It was my mom who gave me the idea and Girasol, too. And I swear, it's Miss Hamilton's fault. She pushes me too far.

It's been five days since my mom left us on our own. Wow. Five days. I've put a lot of work into my calendar page. Today is Wednesday, the due date, and I'm pretty excited because I know my calendar page is one of a kind. It's still a secret, so I can't put the drawing in here for you to see. Not that I don't trust you, but I'm being paranoid. I have loads of clever sayings in speech bubbles next to the heart's labels. For example, You Pump Me Up, and the speech bubble is a barbell—you know, the kind you work out with. Are you visualizing like we talked about before?

Anyway, I ran out of my red colored pencil at home, and Miss Hamilton has a bunch on the counter in our classroom. I need to finish the shading on the right ventricle. I'm getting right to work since today at ten o'clock Mrs. Abernathy is collecting the pages. From the corner of my eye, I see Miss Hamilton stop by Abiola's desk and smile. Out of the corner of my ear, I hear Miss Hamilton droning on.

"Let's put our name at the top, shall we, Rafe?"

"Beautiful job on your homework, Abiola."

"Sandro?"

I snap to attention and hide the contest page in my desk. Usually Miss Hamilton starts writing the daily assignments on the board after she collects the homework. I scan the room. No one else is paying any attention except Abiola, and she is staring at me with a smug expression on her face, sitting with her legs together crisscrossed at the ankles and her hands folded on her desk. The perfect princess. I send subliminal messages to her through the airwaves. *Tattletale*, the messages say.

"Do you have your missing assignments to turn in?"

Well, Cheese Whiz. Remember I told you I had some important things to do? You forgot, too, didn't you? Those missing assignments weren't going any-where, but the calendar page and the two hundred dollars—I mean, deadlines are deadlines.

"My mom told me students have two weeks to complete missing assignments according to the school's homework policy."

Honestly, where do I come up with this stuff? This is a bad lie for two reasons. One, my mom never argues with teachers, so Miss Hamilton will automatically be suspicious. And two, if Miss Hamilton calls my house, she'll know I'm lying. But wait, since my mom is now in Mexico, it will be impossible for them to discuss Sandro the liar. And then it comes to me. Who will answer the phone? My dad. And Sandro the liar will become Sandro the boy who is grounded forever.

"Let's see what you're working on instead of the missing assignments, shall we?" And horror of horrors, she lifts up my desktop and removes the calendar page. I stop myself from yanking it right out of her hand. "No!" I shout. "That's for Mrs. Abernathy."

"Well, Sandro, you should finish your missing assignments before you work on extracurricular proj-ects." She walks near the trash can and my heart stops, but instead of throwing my paper away, she slides my masterpiece into a file folder on her desk.

Ten o'clock comes, and I raise my hand. Miss Hamilton ignores me.

"Line up for art," she says.

"Miss Hamilton," I begin.

"No, Sandro."

I'm steaming mad as we head down to art. I make sure to step in front of Abiola just as she gets to the door so she crashes into me. "Ow," I yell loudly.

"Go to the end, Abiola," Miss Hamilton says.

Abiola flares her nostrils and dramatically brushes my germs off her sparkly T-shirt.

Mrs. Abernathy collects all the entries. Miguel is very secretive about his drawing, but I can see a flash of brilliant colors jump from his page as he sneaks it from between two sheets of paper.

All day long, I'm thinking about how to get back at Miss Hamilton for taking away my drawing and ruining my chance at getting two hundred dollars. I just want to play a little trick on her. Nothing too mean. I *could* put Franklin in my desk for the next time she goes snooping around . . .

Wait a second. What's better than a live turtle? A cat. And what's even better than that? A dead cat. And we both know where I can get a dead cat, don't we?

I rush home after school since I don't have to wait for Girasol anymore. I'm not in the mood for chatty Marta and sneaky Miguel with his secret calendar page. Dad is out with the truck, but when he comes home, I'll be ready. My fingers are crossed.

•

"How was school?" he says. "Keep out of trouble?"

"Yep."

"Really? Your teacher called."

"Just a misunderstanding. See?" I hold up the packet of homework I've been working on since I walked in the door. "Want to check it?"

My dad thumbs through it, not looking it over too carefully. "Give this to your teacher. Tomorrow. Understand?"

"Papi, I want to help with the animals tonight. It's a perfect night, no?"

"I don't think so, Sandro. Too late for a school night."

"We can eat in the truck. I made sandwiches. Look."

My dad gets a funny look on his face. Sad and happy at the same time. Like he's missing my mom but super glad I'm here. He punches my arm. "Okay. We'll see."

After four or five scrap pickups, we go to Crusher, Inc. We eat in the truck while we wait in line. The sandwiches have the jam oozing between two layers of peanut butter. They're messy, but it's just the way me and my dad like it. We eat the little bags of pepitas and drink our Mexican sodas. Both lime flavored. The last two left. We haven't gone to the grocery store since my mom left.

It's getting shadowy by the time we're done at the scrap yard, and I can see my breath. On frosty nights lots of poor critters have trouble crossing the road. Just like I thought—a perfect night.

My dad drives slowly out of town and tells me to keep my eyes open. He knows a couple of roads that border the parks, and sure enough, I spot a couple of dead raccoons within twenty minutes. I mostly stay in the truck, listening to the radio, while my dad shovels the remains into the back onto a tarp.

My dad usually finds lots of squirrels and raccoons, but also deer, opossums, groundhogs, and even vultures that are so focused on picking at the dead animals that they forget to fly away when cars round corners. There's a lesson there. Pay attention, even when you're trying to eat to survive.

The only thing that really bothers my dad is finding people's pets. He hates that. I wonder if that's why he won't let us get a cat or a dog. Thinking about pets reminds me of Franklin, and that reminds me of Girasol, and then my mom pops into my head and that makes me sigh. I've never been without my mom before. It sort of makes you appreciate all the stuff moms do, even though they remind you about chores and manners, too. Don't get me wrong. Dad and I can manage without Mamá, and it's nice in the truck, just me and my dad, the men of the family, out working. I think my dad must like my company cuz he's still heading away from town in search of roadkill.

I don't know how I'm going to snag one of the animals away from my dad, seeing as how I'm pretty sure he keeps track of how much money he will get at the end of the night. I'm hoping for a brainstorm or a stroke of luck, and then I see a blob on the road. I point. My dad pulls over and gets out to investigate. We are far away from the lights of town. I can almost touch the dark, and while my dad's up ahead, his giant shadow in the truck headlights kind of creeps me out.

I decide this might be a good time to go around back and borrow one of his squirrels for my revenge project, since I'm pretty sure we're just about done collecting for the night. I open my door and—I'll be a monkey's uncle—right there, next to my door, is a dead cat. My luck is back.

Yes, I'm a double-crosser and a cheat. But don't you agree with me that Miss Hamilton deserves it? By the time I'm done hiding my revenge cat behind the seat under the empty lunch bags, I see my dad walking back to the truck with another cat on his shovel. *Well, that's sad,* I think. *Those two cats must have been friends with the same not-so-bright idea.*

My dad and I head toward the sanitation department, and he takes care of business.

"Good work, Sandro," Dad says, and suddenly I feel very guilty. When I go to bed that night, I have a hard time sleeping. I keep dreaming Girasol is holding baby kittens crying for their mother.

My dad is still sleeping when I get ready for school and load my little pay-you-back into a plastic bag. I know exactly where Miss Hamilton parks her car. When I get to school, the coast is clear. I sneak between the cars and keep an eye on the building's windows. I think most of the teachers hang out in the workroom first thing in the morning, getting stuff ready to keep their students busy, so they probably won't spy me.

I put on my gloves and transfer the poor cat to Miss Hamilton's windshield. It has gone a little stiff during the night, and I have to keep popping up to straighten it and then duck down to be sure no one is watching. When I finish, at first I'm proud of the way the cat looks as though it just landed, *shplunk*, on her windshield, and then I'm a little ashamed because it's really a mean thing to do.

Oh well. I get in line. I see Miguel. I suddenly remember soccer practice. Cheese Whiz. I can't keep it all straight.

"Why you miss practice? We wait for you." Miguel's really been working on his English. He still misses some of those little things—like the "did" and the "ed" chunk. But it's pretty good, don't you think?

I feel worse. I totally forgot that Miguel picks me up for soccer now. And there are only two and a half weeks until the first playoff game. "I had to help my dad," I say.

Miguel shakes his head and the bell rings. From my seat in the second row from the back, I can see the cars in the parking lot, and I can see the outline of a cat on the windshield of a purplish-red Ford. It's hard to do, but I keep my eyes on my own work so I won't look suspicious.

I'm on the second page of math facts when I hear Abiola sing out, "Miss Hamilton, isn't that your car?" Every word she says tilts up, and every letter is pronounced perfectly. I hate how she sounds so know-it-all and sing-songy all the time.

My heart is now racing. I can already hear Miss Hamilton scream. Maybe she will faint. Take that, you mean teacher. That's what happens when you mess with Sandro the artist. I look casually out the window. My heart stops. Two police officers, Mr. Smalley, and the custodian are surrounding the car. You can't even see the cat, but I can tell they are lifting it off the windshield just by the way they are bending toward the car. A few minutes later, the police car drives off.

"Oh my. What was that about? Let's get back to work, shall we?"

I have the most rotten luck. Everything I do goes wrong. I won't be kicking any goals in our soccer game seeing as how I missed practice again. I won't be winning any art contest seeing as how my entry is in Miss Hamilton's desk. I won't be returning Franklin to Lincoln Elementary seeing as how me and my dad are big fat softies. And I won't be an inventor or an EMT seeing as how I'll probably be arrested for vandalizing Miss Hamilton's car. Worst of all, she didn't even scream, not even one little tiny *ay*. I'm a liar, a cheater, and a thief.

I miss my mom.

There's a knock at the door, and Miss Hamilton goes to open it. I can hear Mr. Smalley's loud whisper.

"Nothing to worry about. Just some prank, I'm sure. No damage to the car."

"What happened?"

"No concern of yours. Do you have any students who might be holding a grudge, though? Wanting to retaliate for anything? Angry about something?"

They both scan the room. I suddenly pretend to be very happy. There's a big fake smile on my face while I pretend to happily do my math computation. I'm practically beaming. And when I look up and Miss Hamilton catches my eye, I manage to give her a friendly wink. Angry? Not me. Not ever.

At recess Miguel motions me over to play soccer, and I pretend not to see him. I squat down by the edge of the wall where nobody can see or bother me and feel very sorry for myself. I watch the soccer ball careening back and forth, a mob of multicolored jackets running helter-skelter after it. I know what the coach would say. "Stay in your positions. Set up the play. Quit chasing the ball. You aren't peewee soccer players."

I'm starting to get a little chilly when a familiar annoying voice chimes by my ear.

"I know who is going to win the calendar contest."

It's Abiola. Cheese Whiz. Doesn't she ever stop with her smarty-pants chatter? I ignore her.

"I forgot my hat, so I went back in, and I heard Mrs. Abernathy tell Miss Hamilton. Guess who it is?" Her voice reminds me of a squeaky rocking chair.

I keep ignoring her.

"You'll be surprised. Want me to tell you?"

I stand up and start to walk away. The side flaps on her fluffy white polar bear hat waggle as she tilts her head. I kind of want to pull on those polar bear ears, but the polar bear is an endangered species.

She calls after me. "Miss. Hamilton turned your calendar page in for you, by the way."

I turn slowly. "And?"

"And you won. Congratulations." Her perfect teeth glint at me from her sickly sweet smile. She wraps the polar bear flaps around her chin and walks away with her thick black braid swinging like a cat's tail.

My throat is dry. I don't think I can breathe. I'm in shock. Miss Hamilton? Miss Hamilton saved me? Mean and spiteful me?

There's a little air under my gym shoes, about two inches at least, and when the bell rings, I'm kind of floating into line. The world sure is a great place. I've decided most of the money I win will have to go to my parents for Girasol instead of that awesome bike I wanted. But then people will see me as the hometown hero. "Can you believe it? He sacrificed his own prize for his sister's surgery," they'll say. Maybe I'll just keep ten dollars for myself. Or maybe twenty since ten dollars hardly buys anything. I can't wait to go inside, so I get in line before the bell even rings.

The afternoon speeds by. I smile at Miss Hamilton every time she says, "Shall we?" I think, *Yes, we shall.* Why did I ever think that phrase was so annoying? I sit straighter and write neater than I've ever written in my life. I raise my hand to answer every question she asks.

I am in reconciliation mode. I know, hard word again, but just think of it as being sorry and trying to make amends. I hope Girasol gets Miss Hamilton for fourth grade. Maybe I will discuss it with Miss Hamilton and she can personally put my little sister on her class list. It's 2:55 p.m. and the end of the day announcements will start at any minute.

"Shhhh," I tell the class. "The announcements."

"Good afternoon, boys and girls. Remember to take the newsletters home to your parents tonight. This week we've been working on hallway behavior. Keep up the good work. And now, here's Mrs. Abernathy with a very special announcement."

I'm on the edge of my seat. Abiola is sitting straight as an arrow, staring at me, grinning like a maniac. Miss Hamilton's hands are clasped together. I can't see Miguel because he sits behind me, and I'm so frozen I can't move.

"Congratulations to everyone who entered the drawing contest. The calendar will be a huge success. The winners for each month are: September—Josiah Watson; October—Simone Davidson; November—Angelica Ariola; December—James Joyner; January—Abiola Khan; February—Miguel Cervantes . . ."

Mrs. Abernathy keeps talking, but I quit listening. There must be a mistake. Abiola heard Mrs. Abernathy tell Miss Hamilton that I won February. My hand starts to leave my desk. I'm forming the words: *There's been a mistake* . . . and then I realize what Abiola did to me. For now, I can't move. But when I thaw out, I'm going to get back at her. For now I just keep telling myself, *Don't cry. I will not cry.*

Miguel is standing next to me. "I'm sorry, Sandro. Your drawing would win if Miss Hamilton turn it in."

I hear my dad's voice, "Be the better man, Sandro."
I gulp down the lump in my throat, and it tastes like
sour milk.

"I can't wait to see your drawing, Miguel. Bet
it's great."

And we walk down the hall to the display case to
see all the calendar pages hanging up. Miguel's page is
stellar. It is comprised of pieces of a puzzle, six different
February holiday pieces shooting out from a brilliant
red heart in the middle. Valentine's Day, Groundhog
Day, Lincoln's Birthday, Washington's Birthday. And
two holidays I forgot all about. Mexican holidays. Día
de la Candelaria, the day people dress up their statues
of Baby Jesus.

And Constitution Day, which just as you would
think, celebrates Mexico's constitution, written in
1917, because of the Mexican Revolution. Miguel tells
me schools in Mexico are closed that day, which is a
bonus. I'm thinking we should probably find out the
exact day our United States Constitution was written.
Maybe you can research that for me, since I'm pretty
busy right now. Then write Congress and request that
day be observed as a national holiday. You have one
week. Go.

"Cool," I tell Miguel, and the better-man part of
me means it. Deep in my heart I know Miguel deserves
to win. "Awesome." I punch his arm. Miguel shrugs

and smiles so his nose wrinkles up. I'm glad he's happy. Or the better-man part of me is, anyway. I look a little closer and see he forgot the second *l* in Lincoln. Oh well. It's still a cool drawing.

The teachers are milling around congratulating the students, oohing and ahhing, and I notice lots of them go into the teacher's lounge and come out with sodas. And that's when I get my next money-making brain-storm. *Blam!* The idea slams into me. I can still help my family. I can still be the hometown hero. I can still put a little spending money in my own pocket. And just like that, the old Sandro is back in action.

CHAPTER 6

Lincoln School's Recycling Entrepreneur

All the way home, Miguel is talking and Marta is skipping and singing. I am calculating. Including all the teachers in our school, even the helper teachers and the secretaries, I come up with forty people. And if those forty people have a soda every day of the week, that equals two hundred cans after five days. And at ten cents a can, how much money will I get every week? That's right, compadre. Twenty dollars.

This is how my brainstorm started. First, I see the teachers drinking sodas and throwing them in the trash. Then I see our custodian, Mr. Tomeski, emptying the trash into the dumpster—all those tesoros cascading into oblivion. Who knew the teachers at our school didn't recycle? Not me. But now it is my opportunity. Save the environment. Save my family. Save my spending money.

"Soccer?" Miguel asks when we get to my house.

"Sí, señor!" I have a lot to do, but I'll be ready. My dad already told me he didn't need me to work today. Something about a job interview, but I think he just doesn't want me to miss soccer practice. Not with the big game coming up.

Mrs. Arona left a pot of something on the counter. Neighbors and friends are great, aren't they? And today, this is perfect because I won't have to scrounge around to find something to eat before practice.

At first, right after Mom and Girasol left, I liked grabbing whatever and eating in front of the TV. Just me and my dad, like a couple of bachelors living on the wild side. Then the kitchen got really messy, and the fridge got really empty. I like pizza, but after one solid week of frozen pizza, I was ready for some new grub.

The problem is, my dad is proud. He tells me, "We are Zapotec people. We have always made our own way." But I guess his stomach talked some sense into his Zapotec pride, too. He told Mrs. Arona what had happened with Girasol. Mrs. Arona told some neighbors, and now somebody brings a pot of something over every couple of days. And while we devour it, my dad reminds me that Zapotecs don't like charity.

I wish we had Internet at home. We used to, but we're making do without quite a few luxuries these days. So I make a little graph and get busy with the phone book. I make a list of all the recycling centers and start calling. Crusher, Inc. is out of the question. Too far away. I want the best price and the closest one to school, since I plan on riding the cans over on my bike every week. This will be a surprise for my family. Sandro saves the day.

Some of the companies I call ask to talk to my parents. As if I can't handle a simple business trans-action. But finally after five calls, a really nice lady answers and gives me serious information. She asks if I'm planning on recycling in just one school.

"I wondered if you'll need the recycle unit. It's a special dumpster with a locking bar. You load in the cans until it's full, and then we come and pick them up," she continues.

I know there's a question I should ask, but I'm speechless. How fantastic is that? Then I gather my thoughts. "Is there a charge?"

"No, sir. We offer this for nonprofit organizations and charitable fundraisers. You have to be there when we make the pickup, and we give you a receipt. The four-yard recycle unit holds about twenty-eight gar-bage bags, or we can deliver a larger size if needed."

"So, how much money is that?"

"Well, it varies. Right now, we're paying eighty-seven cents per pound. Remember, don't crush the cans. We won't take them if they're crushed."

I'm pretty sure we get ten cents a can at Crusher, Inc. And it doesn't matter if they're crushed. Getting paid by the pound doesn't seem good to me. Cans don't even weigh very much. On the other hand, there's no way to get all those cans to Crusher, Inc. unless I get my dad involved, and that means ruining the surprise. In the end, I decide that some money is better than no money. "Do you come just once, or can we fill the container up multiple times?"

"Oh, we will come regularly. Weekly if you want. Don't forget, someone has to be there to supervise the pickup and take the receipt, though."

Well, okay, I think. *That's a good deal.* She asks me some more questions. I have to quickly look up the school address in the phone book. It's getting close to soccer time. I sort of stop paying close attention to what she's saying as I get all my soccer gear together. After I hang up, I realize I forgot to ask how I get the money. Do I take the receipt to the recycle place? The words "nonprofit" and "charitable" are rolling around in my head. What did she mean? Oh well. Plenty of time to figure that out.

At soccer practice while we're running drills, I get a little uh-oh hiccup in my chest. Did I need to get permission from Mr. Smalley to put a dumpster on school property? And since we're not on the best of terms, will he even let me?

Then while practicing shooting, I get another hiccup. How much does Girasol's surgery cost? At least a thousand dollars, I'm betting. I'm working the math out in my head, but I seem to be missing some of the information. How many cans fit in a bag? How many cans equal a pound? I should get extra credit for all this mental math I'm trying to do.

I decide to make up some numbers. Let's say one hundred cans fit in a bag. And let's say twenty-five cans equal a pound. Then every bag would weigh four pounds. So twenty-eight bags is about 112 pounds. Stay with me now. I'm rounding the eighty-seven cents to a dollar. Only $112 for all that work? I figure I need to have ten pickups in all to equal a thousand dollars. And I doubt I will collect twenty-eight bags of cans every week.

My shot goes wild, and the coach yells, "Sandro, pay attention!"

I regroup, and when we practice our double whammy play, I execute like a professional. The team cheers. Saturday is the first playoff game. We will win. I feel it.

I get home and eat dinner by myself. My dad still isn't home. I suppose Mrs. Arona is a good cook, but I miss my mom's flavors and special dishes. It's so quiet I can hear Franklin scratching around in his box. Dad keeps asking me if I think we should just return him to school.

"But Girasol . . ." I always say.

"Yes, I know, but . . ." he always says, and neither one of us wants to make a decision.

Anyway, tomorrow I have to ask Mr. Smalley about the cans, so tomorrow is definitely *not* the day to sneak Franklin back to Lincoln Elementary.

I'm daydreaming when a knock on the door makes me catapult out of my chair, fluttering my homework across the room. I jump up to turn the TV down and hope it's not a burglar being polite. Mrs. Arona enters the unlocked door before I can even take two steps.

"Your papi call me. He is to work tonight." Then she finishes telling me in Spanish that once she puts her kids to bed, she will come and rest on our couch until my dad gets home. Apparently he really did have an interview and got a job working the night shift at some factory. And that means I will have to wait to see him until the morning when I wake up.

I don't know why this makes me sad, but it does. We need money. Girasol's heart surgery costs a lot. But I feel like a soccer ball that is losing air and can't roll right. *Thud. Thud. Thud.* I'm bumping along.

I finish my homework and do a lousy job on it. Then I dig around in my mom and dad's closet until I find my video game. I'm actually grounded from playing it but whatever. They won't know.

When the phone rings, I know it's my dad.

Sure enough. "Sandro? Mijo?"

"Sí, Papi."

"My night job is at TAICO. You must help out now. Your mother will worry if she knows you are alone."

"Mrs. Arona is coming here. She said she's going to rest here until you get home."

"This is good, Sandro. You are not alone. Or your mother will worry. Do you understand?"

And then I do understand. I'm not supposed to tell anybody he's working the night shift. Not even my mom. Mrs. Arona is ten feet away, so technically I'm not really alone. I can hear the TV on in her house and her husband yelling through the duplex's thin walls.

"Sí, Papi."

"I will see you in the morning, Sandro."

Franklin pokes his head out of his box as I head to bed. I put a carrot in Franklin's box. Maybe Girasol knew I would need company. Maybe that is why she stole Franklin.

"Stay strong and sleep tight. Dream of bugs to bite," I tell Franklin.

I crack myself up.

•

It's strange in the night when I get up to use the bathroom and see Mrs. Arona stretched out on our couch. It's so strange that I can't go back to sleep. Instead, I start thinking about Abiola and how I can get back at her for tricking me about the calendar contest. I also start to plan out what I'll say to Mr. Smalley about my recycling plan. And then I have to tell Franklin to keep it down. He's nocturnal, but really, that's no excuse. I guess I do fall back asleep because the bright day wakes me up.

I don't see my dad in the morning. His boots are by the back entrance and the bedroom door is shut. I don't bother to eat breakfast. Just trudge off to school, feeling a little sorry for myself.

Abiola walks by me to get in line. A couple of girls give her the stink eye. She's wearing a pink sequined cap perched sideways over her braid and a jean jacket that reads APPLE BOTTOMS. I begin enacting my revenge by turning around to Miguel and saying in a very loud hope-everyone-can-hear-me voice, "Do you smell something?"

"Maybe your shoe?" He points and I see something brown sticking to my gym shoe. I zip over to the grass and wipe off my shoe. Honestly, Mrs. Arona should keep her dogs out of my yard. I'll have to try again later.

"Yes, Sandro?" says Miss Hamilton after we are all settled down and she sees I've been raising my hand since what feels like the beginning of time.

"Can I go see Mr. Smalley?"

"Did Mr. Smalley ask to see you?"

"Yes."

"Then of course you may go."

I secretly give myself a high five and start to get out of my seat.

"During recess. That's when Mr. Smalley asks to see students."

I make a little noise that sounds a bit growlish. Miss Hamilton writes my name down on her warning list. I'm not sure, but I think my name might be on that list every day. Some guys are just lucky, I guess. After everyone finishes journal writing, we stack our notebooks on Miss Hamilton's desk and line up for gym. By the time I finish Lincoln Elementary, I will be a professional liner-upper.

Just as Miss Hamilton leads us down the hall, I call out, "Miss Hamilton, I forgot to change my shoes!"

"Hurry up, Sandro. Let's try to remember that next time, shall we?"

Yes, we shall. Especially since I don't even have another pair of gym shoes to change into. Especially if all I really want to do is score revenge on a mean old nasty rat. I sneak back into the room and find Abiola's journal. I flip until I find today's entry:

My Hopes and Dreams . . . I hope my dad changes his mind about transferring me to a private school. Private schools cost a lot of money. I think Lincoln is a good school. If I go to private school I will have to quit playing my favorite game because it costs money, too. My hope for fourth grade is to be the top student all year. My dad wants me to be a doctor, so that is my dream, too. My other dream is to . . .

I stop reading. The page is spotless. No eraser marks. No cross-outs. And the curly writing almost fills the page, but there is just enough room at the bottom for a little. clever forgery. Soon I'm off to gym in my stinky old gym shoes.

Why can't we have gym all day? Everyone loves gym. We learn all kinds of life skills. Teamwork and rules for games we'll play for the rest of our lives. At least we should have it more than just two days a week. The time goes so fast, and before I know it, Miss Hamilton is at the door with a very sour pickle face. Abiola tries to tattle that I skipped her free throw turn at one of the stations in gym on purpose, but Miss Hamilton tells her to put her hand down with the same growl I had in my voice earlier.

This ought to be good, I think. Back in the classroom, Miss Hamilton gives us a math worksheet and invites Abiola out to the hall. Uh-oh, spaghetti-oh, Abiol-oh.

We all hear the yelling when it starts. "How dare you write this about me in your journal?" Miss Hamilton is so mad, and I see her jerking the journal up and down through the door window.

Abiola is crying and shaking her head. I can just see her braid whipping from side to side. "I didn't write that. It wasn't me." Her clipped words sound *rat-a-tat-tat*.

"How dare you lie? This is your journal and your handwriting."

"But I didn't write that."

"In this country teachers are treated with respect. What will your parents say?"

Abiola screams, "They will believe me! I didn't write that. And if you don't believe me, you are a fat cow just like it says."

And then that perfect little princess turns into the Tasmanian Devil. I've never seen anybody go so absolutely berserk. Stamping her feet and waving her arms, gold bracelets flashing in the dim hall.

The last thing we hear her yell is, "Take your hands off me, you mean witch!"

No one in our class moves a muscle. We are all in shock. And when Miss Hamilton opens the door, a feather falling would sound noisier than a firecracker. We're all acting busy, too, especially me, making sure my heart doesn't thump so hard it breaks out of my chest. I am ashamed of myself and pleased at the same time. I didn't plan for such a big spectacle. I didn't figure on Miss Hamilton being so sensitive and Abiola being so infuriated. In-fyur-E-ate-ed. Here's your word lesson. *In* means *into*, at least in this word. So Abiola went *into fury*—she became *infuriated*.

And speaking of Abiola—where is she? I ask Jazzy to find out, so she raises her hand, doing the restroom wiggle routine. She returns and goes behind my desk, whispering, "Not in the hall or girls' bathroom."

I can't wait until recess so I can spy on the Tasmanian Devil in Mr. Smalley's office, where I'm sure she is being held. Maybe she got suspended. Yelling at a teacher? Holy guacamole. I am guiltily gleeful. Serves her right, though, doesn't it?

I'm not happy about missing recess to talk to Mr. Smalley. It's the double whammy. *Bam*—you miss recess. *Wham*—you're in the principal's office. But at least I'm not in trouble. I head up the stairs, past the calendar pages locked up tightly in the glass display case. Good thing they're locked, too, since Abiola's January page taunts me as I walk by. I go right up to the counter in the office and stand on my tiptoes to look taller.

"Excuse me. I'm here to see Mr. Smalley," I say.

"Is he expecting you?" I don't recognize the secretary sitting behind the counter.

Good question. I decide to tell the truth. "No, but I have something to tell him."

"He's busy right now. Have a seat."

Great. I'm going to miss all of recess. And probably lunch. I sit in the chair closest to Mr. Smalley's door. At least I can entertain myself by trying to eavesdrop. Technically, I'm not eavesdropping because I'm not listening at a window or a wall, but I think eavesdrop sounds better than snoop. And it's my lucky day. Mr. Smalley is busy, all right. And guess who is keeping him busy? You got it. Abiola.

"Name? Young man? Hello?"

Whoops. I was paying so much attention to Mr. Smalley's office I didn't hear what the secretary said.

"Sandro."

"Sandro what?" She is tapping a pen impatiently on a sticky-note pad. Seems to me I'm notorious enough to be known even by new secretaries.

"Sandro Zapote."

"Okay. I'll let him know. You can go back to class now."

Oh, no you don't. Not when I'm about to overhear some really good information. And I've already sacrificed most of my recess. This new secretary doesn't understand. Hopefully Mrs. Lopez, my favorite secretary, will come to my rescue. In my sweetest, most convincing angelic voice I say, "Would it be all right if I just waited a little bit longer? It's really important."

And it works. I lock eyes with Mrs. Lopez, who recognizes me. She pipes up and says I can stay, giving me a slight wink. This is great. Through the window in Mr. Smalley's door, I can see the side of Abiola's reddened face and a woman's hand poking out of some gauzy material patting her cheek. Must be her mom. A man is talking with an accent and it's not Mr. Smalley, so it has to be her dad. Abiola is either still crying or trying to stop crying because her neck is jerking up and down, rooster-style.

Abiola's dad says, "You need to be more careful in this school, yes? Abiola has had many troubles here."

Mr. Smalley says, "We have no tolerance for bullying here. I can assure you of that."

Abiola snuffles and lets loose a sob. Her mom says something in another language, and Abiola shakes her head.

"It would be easier to handle this if your daughter gives us the name of the bully who is bothering her."

"She is worried there will be retaliation. Is race bullying a problem at this school?" her father's voice says.

Mr. Smalley's chair makes a loud scraping noise, and he suddenly materializes in front of the door window I'm spying through. He sounds very perturbed. "Absolutely not. This is kids being kids."

"We want the best education for her. Her opportunity to learn must not be wasted. There are other schools, yes? Private?"

Mr. Smalley turns the doorknob. "That will not be necessary, I assure you. I will keep an eye on the situation and discuss actions to be taken with Miss Hamilton." He opens the door. "Thank you for advocating for your daughter."

I'm thinking two things: One, maybe this is not a good time to talk to Mr. Smalley. And two, Abiola is a good faker. As the Kahns come out of the office, I drop my chin down and partially cover my face with my hand, hoping to look deep in thought, hoping they don't see me.

Through a slit between my fingers, I see Mr. Kahn holding his head straight. He has a badge with his picture on it clipped to his suit pocket. It looks like the word TACO is written above his picture. *Nah*, I think. *I'm just getting hungry.* Mrs. Kahn strokes Abiola's braid. Abiola says something in a language I don't understand, then she and her mother turn and look directly at me. Her mother has a scarf around her head and face, so it's just her eyes that convict me. Abiola's mouth scrunches into an I-hope-you-drop-dead sneer, and then they are gone.

"Are you waiting to see me, Sandro?" Mr. Smalley is standing next to his office door. Mrs. Lopez just put a tasty smelling sack from the sandwich shop on his desk.

This is probably a very bad time to ask Mr. Smalley to allow me to become Lincoln Elementary's recycling entrepreneur, which, for your information, means independent business person. He's still red in the face from his conference with Abiola's parents and obviously hungry. But if I come back tomorrow, I will have to wait again and miss more of my lunch and recess time. So I put on my friendly business face and sit down across from him.

"Mr. Smalley, I have a proposition that will benefit both Lincoln Elementary and the environment," I start.

Mr. Smalley nods and taps his fingers together. His eyes travel to his sandwich bag, then back to me.

I continue. "You see, I noticed we have a can problem."

I start explaining, but while I'm talking my train sort of runs off its track, and I can't seem to think straight. I keep seeing the word TACO from Mr. Kahn's shirt, which is the same color and style of the word TAICO on the shirts my dad throws into the laundry basket. I mistakenly say fun-raiser instead of fundraiser, and a fleeting image of me on a brand new bike rides through my brain. I quickly add some stuff about worthwhile projects. I'm suddenly haunted by Mrs. Kahn's spooky eyes accusing me without a word. Mr. Smalley listens, but you can tell he's also preoccupied. I finish with my spiel, and he says, "Very philanthropic of you, Sandro."

So he's one-upping me on the word usage. I've never heard that one before. It could mean stupid or smart or enterprising. But whatever it means, he agrees to my recycling plan. I should be ecstatic. I should be overjoyed. I should be counting my chickens before they hatch.

But instead I have a nagging feeling that I have overlooked an important detail. I'm probably just traumatized by Abiola's mother's eyes and imagining my dad's factory is on Mr. Kahn's badge. And as soon as I get home, I'm checking out what race bullying really is. Something tells me it's not good, and Sandro the brand new first-ever Lincoln Elementary Recycling Entrepreneur will not be want to be involved.

CHAPTER 7

Play Like a Zapotec

S uddenly my simple fourth grade life gets very complicated and full of secrets.

I secretly plan how I will hide the recycling project from my parents until I can present them with a boatload of cash.

I secretly stash the posters I make under Girasol's bed so my dad doesn't see them before I carry them to school.

They're pretty clever, if I say so myself. MAKE EARTH YOUR FAN—RECYCLE THAT CAN. IN YOUR RUSH, PLEASE DON'T CRUSH.

And then there is Sandro the selfish brat who plans to steal some of the recycle money from Sandro the hero for a brand new bike. Shhh, don't tell him.

When my mom calls from Mexico one day, I keep the secret of Papi's night job and pretend we are having lots of father-son bonding time.

"Sí, Mamá. We're eating. We're fine. We miss you, but it's fun, the two of us."

The truth is, I hardly see my dad. He works from four in the afternoon to midnight at the TAICO plant. He calls during his dinner, comes home after I'm in bed, and gets up after I go to school. Mamá tells me that Girasol has to be stronger before she has the surgery. I'm no doctor, but isn't that backward thinking? Won't the surgery make her stronger? When I hang up, little drops of worry start to dribble into my head and my happiness seeps away.

I remember one time when the drain plug on our bathtub got warped. After you filled up the tub, you had to leave the water running, or before you knew it you were sitting in an empty tub. That's how I feel right about now. The water is draining out of me, and some-body keeps turning off the faucet. Will things ever be back to normal, or will my plug always be warped?

My family's secret in the half-shell is still my houseguest. I remember to put a rock in front of my bed-room door when I leave for school in case Frankie the escape artist decides to take a stroll. I'm sure

Mrs. Arona and her yippy Chihuahua would have a lot to say about Sandro and the stolen turtle. So the rock is also my secret spy technique for nosy neighbors.

I'm trying to keep things neat and tidy at home, not only because I promised my mom I'd take care of my dad, but also so Mrs. Arona will not feel too sorry for us. I know my mom will hate to hear that everyone is helping out poor Peony Zapote who is in Mexico with her sick daughter. As I sweep the kitchen floor, I have to admit, it's amazing how much dirt two guys can generate each week.

Oh, and there's one more secret. Race bullying is not a good thing; it's very serious. And truthfully, that is not what I was doing to Abiola. I don't like Abiola because she is an annoying tattletale who is ruining my life but not because she is from a different country. Of course, that's hard to prove, so I have to make sure no one ever finds out it was me who wrote that stuff about Miss Hamilton in her journal.

In line one day after recess, I ask Abiola where her dad works, and yep, you guessed it. He works at TAICO. More bad luck for me. And I don't know for sure, but I imagine her dad is some head honcho bossing my dad around. Which makes me dislike her even more.

I sure hope my dad never runs into Abiola's dad at TAICO and starts talking about Lincoln Elementary. You know how it goes. First, they'll find out that their wonderful kids are in the same class. And then they'll find out that yes, indeed, Sandro Zapote is that same Sandro who pushed Abiola in third grade and is now accused of race bullying her in fourth grade. And then next thing you know, my dad will mysteriously lose his job, and it will be my fault.

Keeping all this stuff straight, getting all my homework done, making it to soccer practice, and remembering to eat and shower makes me feel older than my eleven years. I'm so tired when my head hits the pillow at night, it's adiós, Sandro. I sure used to have a lot more fun before Mamá and Girasol went to Mexico. But I try not to think about that too much.

•

The day of our playoff game—Saturday—I wake up early. I've been collecting cans from the teachers' lounge and the lunchroom for a week now. I pitched what seems like thousands of cans into the dumpster. After Mr. Smalley put details about the recycling program in the announcements at the beginning of the week teachers started bringing their soda cans from home. Big bags full. They don't get any benefit from waste management, so they figured why not help out an enterprising entrepreneur? Remember that word entrepreneur? I've been too tired lately to worry about your vocabulary. And Mr. Tomeski talked to his custodian friends at other schools and talked them into giving us their cans. So the dumpster is full and ready to be dumped.

I figured out the exact answer for the recycling estimation problem. Twenty-eight cans equal a pound. Each trash bag holds roughly 128 cans. Each bag is worth about four dollars, and there's at least thirty bags in the dumpster, so I figure around $120 will be my take. Not bad for one week. Plenty of money for Girasol and other secret expenses. Eat your heart out, contest winners Miguel and Abiola. Soon your two hundred dollars will look like pennies compared to my riches.

Before my dad can wake me up to go to the game, I sneak out of the house, riding my old bike to school. There I meet the driver from the recycling center, get the receipt, and fly back home to get ready. Cheese Whiz, I'm only eleven, and my life is a mess. I am in such a rush I forget to ask the driver about cashing in the receipt. *No problem,* I think. *Next week I'll make sure to ask.*

My dad is quiet on the way to the game. Tired probably. I feel the same way. It's the end of October. It's chilly-cold. Halloween is right around the corner. I was a soccer player last year for trick-or-treating. I took Girasol, the princess in pink, around the block. Maybe this year I'll go as a recycling collector. That was a joke. Not funny, huh? I think I've lost my sense of humor. I know I've lost my edge.

On soccer game days, my mom would always make me a special breakfast. "For luck, Mijo," she'd say. She would iron my jersey and shorts and fill my jug with ice and water. On the way to the field, Papi would always tell us stories of his fútbol days in Mexico. "Play like a Zapotec," he always said to me before I took the field before a big game.

Today, nada, zippo, zero. No special breakfast; I eat cereal. No perfect uniform—it's not even clean. And I can't find my jug, so I grab a bottle of water from the fridge. I tell myself that if my dad says, "Play like a Zapotec," I will be okay. The team is already out practicing as we pull up. I'm not late, am I? I streak off to join them before I realize he didn't say it. I tell myself, "Play like a Zapotec." It's not the same.

"You're late, Sandro." The assistant coach—Noel's dad—is putting the soccer bags in a perfect row.

"How come?"

"Playoff game. Coach wants everyone here an hour early."

Well, shoot. I must have missed that memo. My mom always keeps track of those details. I want to say, *Give me a break, would you?*

"Lap it."

Cheese Whiz. If I lap it, I'll be too tired to play. Coach is busy running drills on the field. No way would he approve of this, but if I refuse, I could be benched.

There's something called solidarity between coaches even when they don't agree. I take a deep breath and start running around the field. My dad lifts his palms up, asking me without words, "What in the world?" I shrug and keep going.

The game starts, and I'm on the field. I'm streaking down the sideline, but the pass is intercepted. I rush back to help out. Our goalie boots it to Black Hole Noel. I streak again. He passes it wide, and I can't catch it. Wow! Their defender has a flip throw-in, and the ball practically scales the entire field. That's not good. By the first substitution, my side hurts and I haven't even touched the ball. I'm the monkey in the middle of a huge keep-away game.

"Sandro, you've got to get to the ball. Get your foot on it. Noel, pass it to his feet. Miguel, move forward and stop hanging back."

I drink most of my water. By the end of the first half, I have been effectively ineffective. I'm not on my game. My passes aren't crisp. My throw-ins are hesitant. Worst of all, it's not even Noel's fault. To his credit, he tried to pass to me, and I messed it up.

"I'm sorry, Sandro, we've got to try something else." The coach points at the bench, and I sit. I look over at my dad. I can tell he's disappointed with my performance. When the game starts back up, he yells just as hard for Cesar—my replacement—as he did for me. When Noel scores, my dad goes bonkers with all the other fans. I close my eyes and wish I was back in bed asleep, and while I'm peacefully daydreaming, the other team scores. The yelling wakes me up. Noel's dad tells me to stand up if I can't stay awake.

The ref blows the whistle. The game is over, and it's tied. He explains the overtime rules. Two ten minute overtimes and then five penalty kicks. The coach comes over and asks us to huddle.

"Sandro, I want you to be on the field at the end of the second overtime, or you won't be eligible to kick any penalty shots," he says.

I feel a little better. I may still have a chance to redeem myself.

"Remember now, boys, this is double elimination. Even if we lose this game, we have another shot. If we win this game, we advance. What do you want to do?"

We all shout, "WIN THIS GAME!"

It's still tied after the first overtime. Miguel gives me a fist pump. Me and my tired body lope out to the field for the second overtime. I've been out of water since the first half, but I don't want to say anything. I'm a proud Zapotec, and we don't take charity. I know I have to make up for my poor showing, so I generally make a nuisance of myself. I grab shirts, stick my leg out and trip somebody, then slide tackle the good throw-in guy. Finally, the ref blows his whistle and gives me a yellow card.

I tone it down a bit. The second overtime ends. We're still tied. *That's good,* I think. My dad has his head bent backward with both hands covering his face. The coach is shaking his head with his eyes closed. What is the matter with everybody? We've practiced penalty kicks until we're blue in the face. This is a piece of cake.

We line up. Five players on our side. Five players on their side. Here we go. Score for them. Score for us. Score for them. Score for us. Miss for them. Here's our chance. But it's Noel. And you guessed it. Not even close to the goal. Miss for us. Then they score, and we score. Their last guy is up. It's the really good throw-in player. Of course he scores.

And now, yours truly is up. Watch and learn, amigos. I hold the ball. I whisper to it, "I am a proud Zapotec." I set it down in the penalty box. I back up. I put up my hand. I hear my dad yell, "Play like a Zapotec!" and my heart feels as big as a balloon. Then I'm off like the wind. I connect. The ball sails. I'm in slow motion, watching as my redemption sails right into the . . . hands of the goalie. The other team erupts with joy, and I slink back to the bench. The last thing I want to do is say good game and high-five our victors. Whoever made up that stupid rule?

Our coaches gather us together and tell us a bunch of stuff. No one is responsible, blah, blah, blah. We play as a team. We win as a team. We lose as a team. Yah? Well, maybe neither of my coaches missed their redemption penalty shot before. One person. One shot. One giant miss.

Miguel catches up to me as I drag myself to the truck.

I want to say, "I'm sorry, I blew it," but I can't.

"Sandro, you have a good kick. The goalie is just having a lucky day. Somebody else is not having luck." He points to the middle row of cars, and I see Noel. Head down. Getting yelled at by his dad. And his dad is poking him in the chest every time he says the word *you*.

Miguel and I raise our eyebrows at each other. Yikes, it's just a game. And yet, I have that same satisfied feeling watching Noel get yelled at as when Abiola got in trouble with Miss Hamilton. I'm developing a pattern of being happy when others get what I think they deserve. Maybe it's a personality defect. But right away, I feel guilty about being happy and start feeling sorry.

Miguel tugs on my jersey and nods his head toward Noel. "Come on."

"Are you nuts?" I stay planted next to Dad's truck. Sometimes Miguel is dense. I mean, who cares about Noel? Besides that, it's not our business, and it might make it worse for him.

Miguel sets his soccer ball down and starts to dribble through the parking lot. The ball goes wild and lands between Noel and his dad. I can't hear anything, but I see Noel pick up the ball and give it to Miguel. Miguel sticks his hand out to Noel's dad and shakes it. Then he slaps Noel a high five and walks away. Noel's dad sort of pats Noel on the back and gets into the car. All this happens in a nanosecond, of course, but I feel a puff of pride that Miguel is my friend and a puff of disgrace that I don't deserve him. Me, the traitor, happy about Noel getting blasted by his dad about a game—yes, an important playoff game, but still just a game.

In the truck on the way home, my dad says, "You've played better."

"I'm just tired."

"I'm sorry I have to work, Mijo."

I'm in shock. Did he just say he's sorry? It's the first time those words have crossed his lips. This is a dark day for the Zapotec people.

"It's okay, Papi."

"Next game, better luck."

•

Monday comes way quicker than it ever has. I'm already tired of this recycling project. Is this how my dad feels every day after work? If Miss Hamilton wants to know what my dad does for a living now, I'll tell her he's killing himself for a living. He picks up his scrap metal tesoros without me before he goes off to his night shift job, and during his dinner hour he shovels up poor dead animals.

"We collect candy tonight?" Miguel asks as we walk to school.

"Trick or treat? Yep. Tonight. What are you going to be?"

"A bullfighter, I think. With my dad's sombrero and red fabric." He does a little bullfighter move. "And you?"

"A soccer player."

Marta stops skipping ahead and says, "You can't be a soccer player. You're already a soccer player."

"So? I was a soccer player last year, and it was fine."

"I'm going to be a baby," Marta says.

"You can't be a baby. You're already a baby," I say back.

"Not nice, Sandro." And she kicks me with her pointed toe shoes. Ow. That hurts.

"You can be my toro. I have the piñata from last birthday. Remember? The bull?"

I don't want to hurt his feelings, but walking around with part of a piñata on my head would be worse than actual bullfighting.

Even though it's almost November, it's not cold enough for us to wait inside for the bell to ring. The days start out chilly, but I know by recess it will be perfect soccer weather. I'm still feeling bad about the penalty kick, so I'm just about to suggest that Miguel practices with me when a little commotion grabs my attention. Kids are running over to take a look at something near the bike rack.

Miguel and I push through the third graders to get a look. The flames on the frame blaze into my eyes. Then I see the shock absorbers on the T-bone, the Shimano Revo 21-Speed Twist Shifters, and the Tektro brakes. It's the most amazing, awesome, super-fantastic bike I've ever seen.

In fact, it's the very one I planned to buy if I won the two hundred dollars in the calendar contest. The very one Sandro the selfish brat is still thinking about buying with Sandro the hero's recycle money. I'm overcome with greed and avarice and covetousness and rapacity and every other word that means I want it and I want it bad. Who is this cool kid riding this cool bike?

Miguel is poking me. And poking me. And poking me. I'm way too busy imagining myself coasting down to River's Edge and tricking out in the skate park to pay him any attention. "Cut it out," I snap at him.

"Sandro, look."

The cool kid turns, and the bike helmet comes off. No, it can't be.

I'm barreling back to earth from my imaginary world. I'm crashing into my greed and avarice. It's not fair. She carefully pulls the bike into the bike rack and winds a ginormous cable in a perfect spiral around the wheel and over the flames. She rotates the combination and checks it twice. Then she shakes her wrists, her gold bracelets gleaming in the sun, and picks up her pink backpack.

"Hi, Sandro. Hi, Miguel."

I am unable to speak. I have been struck by a lightning bolt of jealousy.

Miguel recovers. "That new bike is yours?"

"Yes. My daddy got it for me. To make me happy again."

I cannot speak. I cannot move. I cannot breathe. My fourth-grade life flashes before my eyes. My trip to the principal's office. My trip to the hall. My February calendar page. My failed attempts at getting revenge. My dad getting a phone call about my homework. I will never be happy again. And it's all thanks to Abiola.

That's it. The war is on, and it has nothing to do with race bullying. Somehow I will figure out a way to buy a bike that's even better than Abiola's and to help my family pay for Girasol's surgery. Sandro the selfish brat will have to make a deal with Sandro the hero. I will make everyone happy—even me. I am filled with glorious purpose, as the Avengers would say.

CHAPTER 8

Never Bite the Hand That Feeds You

I manage to control myself all day on Monday. No sense getting grounded on Halloween. I rush home and wait for Miguel and Marta. There's a knock on the door.

"Waaaa! Trick or treat," says Marta. Her hair is in a ponytail that sprouts up from the top of her head. Her shoulders are wrapped in a fluffy pink blanket, and she's holding a pacifier.

"Sorry, I don't have any baby food," I tell her.

"You're supposed to give me candy."

"I don't have any candy either."

"If you don't have candy, then I trick you."

"Okay. Trick me."

"But I don't know any tricks." Marta stomps her foot and starts to cry.

"Oh, never mind. I'll give you my first piece of candy when I get it, okay?" I grab my candy bag and close the door.

"My mom made me bring her." Miguel throws up his hands.

It's slow going because of Marta, but in the end we get plenty of candy because people think she's cute and that it's nice we're taking her around. I'm sorry Girasol missed Halloween. She wanted to be a black cat this year.

After trick-or-treating, I sort my candy and make a nice pile for Girasol. I'm more of a chocolate fan, and she likes the gummy stuff. I debate where to put the full-sized Skittles package because, technically, they're not chocolate or gummy. In the end, I rip them open and eat them, so I don't have to decide.

It rains Tuesday and Wednesday, and I'm a drowned rat by the time I get the icy wet combination lock open on the dumpster and harrumph five bags over the side. Some nice teacher donated a tall garbage can for the teacher's lounge, so every day I pick up one bag in there and four bags in the lunchroom—all full to the top with cans. Who knew people drank so much soda?

It's still raining when I wake up Thursday and walk to school. Everything is gloomy and gray, including my mood. Maybe I'm causing the weather. I do notice that Abiola (aka the poor princess) hasn't ridden her bike all week, and that makes a little bright spot in my mind. The hallway is a disaster. Mr. Tomeski will sure have a big job mopping up the muddy mess. I sit down at my desk in my damp jeans, and Miss Hamilton places a letter in front of me addressed to my parents. Now what? I stuff the letter into my take-home folder and try to forget about it.

The sky clears up just before recess. Some men in white polo shirts with a logo over the pocket are measuring the playground. New equipment is long overdue. Maybe a tube slide and one of those bridges with the rope loops. Not for us soccer players but for the little kids.

Miguel helps me with the bags of cans after school. I think he partly sticks around because he's afraid I will forget about soccer practice with my new responsibility as recycle coordinator.

"Wow. Lots of cans. Too much work, Sandro," he says.

"Yah." I decide I'm going to tell him about my Sandro the hero plan on the way to soccer practice. We both care about our families. Just after Miguel got the check for the calendar prize, I asked him how he spent

it, and Marta jumped in and informed me he gave all
the money to his mom.

"Miguel loves our family," she said.

"She's borrowing it to pay the bills, that's all,"
Miguel said and then told Marta to quit blabbing.

I love my family, too, so I'm going to give them the
money I make from the recycling program. Well, almost
all of it, that is. And they don't even have to pay me back.

The dumpster is so full that I climb up on the lid
and stomp it down. The cans and the money are adding
up faster than I thought they would. Maybe the whole
world wants to help me out. I feel a little humble and
annoyed at myself for being jealous and selfish, wishing
the money didn't have to pay for Girasol's surgery but
instead could all be mine to buy whatever I want.

From up here on top of the dumpster, I can see
the whole school grounds. Marta is waiting for me and
Miguel on the sidewalk, trying to close her umbrella. A
big girl stops to help her, but it looks stuck or something.
Wait a sec. She's walking away with the girl. I can only
see their backs. She's not supposed to do that.

"Miguel! Miguel!" He must have gone back into the
school for the last few bags because I can't see him any-
where. So I leap off the dumpster and chase after Marta.

"Marta!" She might not know about stranger
danger, so I run as fast as I can through the swarms of
kids and parents. I'm still a penalty shot away from her

when a woman walks around the front of her car and stoops next to Marta.

"No!" I shout and charge on. The woman is taking Marta's umbrella. The girl is taking her backpack. What are they doing? Are they trying to give her a ride? Are they kidnapping her? Marta is too little to know what to do. What should I do? Stop, drop, and roll is for fires. You call 911 for emergencies. Get the license plate number? Yes, that's it. But once she's in the car, it'll be too late.

"Stop!" I scream. "Don't touch her."

The woman looks up, and the girl turns around. I'm close enough now to see the eyes peering over at me. They drill into my forehead. The woman's scarf is under her neck and not over her face this time. Then I see Abiola take the umbrella from her mom and place it into Marta's backpack. The scarf goes back up over Abiola's mom's face.

I'm close enough now to hear Marta say, "Thank you," while Abiola helps her put on her backpack and then straightens the straps. "Your mom is nice. Is her face cold?"

"No, she's wearing a hijab. She wears it for her religion." When Abiola says this, she looks at me.

I try to defend myself. "I'm sorry. I couldn't see. I thought your mom was kidnapping Marta. I mean, not kidnapping, but sort of taking her home, and I mean, we didn't know and so . . ." My voice trails off.

Abiola shakes her head, disgusted by my mistake. She gets into the backseat of the car. I watch it pull away from the curb.

I hear Miguel yelling my name. I wave to him, and when he runs over I explain to him that Marta almost got into Abiola's car.

"Don't run off with people you don't know," he tells her.

"I know her. She's Sandro's girlfriend."

Talk about disgusting.

"And she's nice," Marta adds.

"No, she's not," I say.

"Nicer than you," she says back.

Wow. I'm arguing with a six year old. I've stooped to a new low. Miguel points to the bags of cans he's left by the dumpster before he heads home, pulling Marta along with him.

"Be ready for soccer," he says as I head back to the dumpster.

•

My house is quiet and boring as I sit there waiting for Miguel to pick me up for soccer. How many weeks until it's back to normal? Even Franklin seems down, brown as the bark in his box. I pick out the old veggies and put in fresh ones, along with a strawberry. My dad brings Frankie a little something from the salad bar where he eats every night. Sometimes he mentions Franklin going back to school, but he's not serious. I think in his heart he believes Franklin gives Girasol (and maybe us, too) hope—hope that she will make it through the surgery and be back home to see her beloved turtle again.

"Go ahead, Frankie," I tell him. "Enjoy. Soon enough you'll be back on turtle rations."

I eat a tortilla spread with peanut butter and some Halloween candy while I watch TV. After I clean up, I see a letter addressed to me laying on the table, and it reminds me of the letter in my backpack, which I'll probably "forget" to give my dad until after the weekend's over. This letter, though, is from my mom, and when I open it, I see two drawings from Girasol.

One picture is me playing soccer and the ball is bigger than my head. I hope that's not a bad sign that the playoff game will be too big for me to handle. The other picture is of four people and a turtle, so I guess that's our family with Franklin. The girl in the pink shorts is the tallest, and the boy with the jet black hair covering his eyes is the shortest.

I try not to infer any hidden meaning from the drawing, but I keep thinking how small and unimportant she's made me. I wonder if it's a bad omen. Like maybe no matter how hard I try, I will never accomplish anything in life. Cheese Whiz. I'm losing it. It's a silly drawing by my kindergarten sister who doesn't even know how to draw proportions.

Mamá's letter is written all in Spanish, which is good because it helps me hear her voice; but it's also bad because reading Spanish is difficult for me.

> *Sandro, mijo. We are fine. Girasol is fine. We are waiting for the surgery. Everyday Abuelo takes us to see the animals. Girasol loves the horse, Paco. Remember Paco? When you come to visit, Abuelo says you will be ready to learn to ride. Girasol is chicken of the chickens, so if they're in the yard she won't go outside. It is hot here, not like the fall where you are. I don't think Girasol knows Halloween will be over when she gets home. She is still talking about being a black cat. Maybe she can dress up and you can play trick or treat for her. I know Papi is happy you are there to keep him company, but we all miss you. Abuela wants me to tell you to eat, to be strong, and win at soccer. Be good in school. Te quiero, mijo. Mamá.*

When I'm done reading, it's time for soccer practice, and my nose is all snuffly. I grab a paper towel and dab at the water in my eyes before I blow my nose. Must be all this rain . . .

At soccer practice I have a brand new strategy for connecting with the ball. I visualize Abiola's new bike in the corner of the net, and I've got perfect aim every time. While we practice, I see our two coaches with their heads together marking up their clipboards. For the scrimmage, the coach tries Cesar out as goalie. Not a bad idea. Cesar is small but quick. Coach puts Jared, our regular goalie, in for Noel. Good idea, too. Jared reads the ball really well. But then—I don't believe it—he puts Noel in my position! Me, the Avenger, faster than a speeding bullet, the indomitable right forward. Me, on the bench.

"Relax, Sandro," says my coach. "I'm exploring options. I want to have a couple of cards up my sleeve in case we run into a brick wall in the playoffs."

If he thinks Noel in my position is a card up his sleeve, then he's thinking like a brick wall. Of course, I only nod. Take another tip from me: don't ever argue with a coach. Or as the saying goes, never bite the hand that feeds you. Just look alert. Cheer for your teammates. And if your name is called, jump up like your butt's on fire and get into the game.

Noel's dad seems very pleased with himself. He keeps turning around to stare at me. I act happy as can be. If I can play like a Zapotec, by golly, I can sit like a Zapotec, too. Miguel runs off the field to get a drink and whispers, "Loco," and nods at the coaches. I know I don't have long to wait. We cover for Black Hole Noel in every game. And sure enough, he proves to be just a flash in the pan.

"Sandro," bellows my coach. "Go in for Noel."

Be the better man, I tell myself as Noel marches past me. "Good job, Noel," I say.

Noel holds his head very straight and doesn't look at me. "Lousy passes," he says.

Now this is more like it. With Miguel, Jared, and me on the field, we execute every play with precision. Cesar's kicks aren't powerful, but they are insanely accurate. Jared keeps us moving up and down the field, watching for traffic and negotiating between defenders. Within twenty minutes, I have a hat trick. The team we're scrimmaging doesn't know what brick wall they just ran into.

Coach claps me on the shoulder as we come off the field at the end of the scrimmage. "See, I like that card up my sleeve," he says as he writes something down on his clipboard. I know Saturday he'll be playing my card.

When Papi calls, I tell him about my hat trick.

"That's good, Mijo. We'll make a special breakfast Saturday. A lucky breakfast."

•

Friday is a great day. I'm still contemplating Abiola's demise, like always, but my head is too full of soccer and soda cans to dwell on such trivial matters for long. I do institute the ABC rule, confidentially, of course. If A (Abiola) comes within three feet of Miguel or me, we hold our B (Breath) and C (Cough). I guess Miguel told Jazzy by mistake about the ABC rule, and I might have mentioned it to Lorenzo and Jaylen, too. I don't think Abiola has a clue, and it's kind of funny to hear all the coughing and then breathing out as she walks by any of us.

I'm up super early on Saturday morning, get my uniform and water jug all set, and race on my bike to meet the recycling truck at the school. He's the early bird again, already there waiting for me. Ha! Once I buy my new 21-speed bike, *I* will be the early bird to everything.

Girasol comes before your new bike, Sandro the hero reminds me.

"Big storm coming. You better get home," the driver warns me. I take the receipt, and before I can ask him where I can cash it in, he's in the cab and pulling away. Well, Cheese Whiz. Maybe I'll call the lady at the center and ask her later today.

My hands are freezing, and dark clouds that I swear weren't there ten minutes ago swirl together overhead. Big cold drops hit my head. It's raining and snowing at the same time. Where does my mom keep the winter stuff? Good question. I put the pedal to the metal and make it home in record time.

"Game canceled," my dad greets me with the news and goes back to bed.

Apparently breakfast is canceled, too. When my dad finally gets up for real at ten o'clock, he tells me the league will reschedule the game for sometime this week. He laughs when I show him the pictures Girasol sent me.

I think about the letter in my backpack again. Nah, it can wait. It's probably about parent-teacher conferences or my latest test scores. My dad is very big on academic success. Especially since he's an engineer. And I would sure hate to disappoint him when he's got so much on his mind already. Be sure to chime in here if you agree.

I'm still in bed on Sunday morning when the phone rings. My dad busts through my door and grabs me and dances around the room. "Girasol will have surgery this week. This week. Get dressed. We will go to light a candle at mass."

So far I know very little about what is happening. Bits and pieces. Girasol and my mom are with my abuelos in Oaxaca. The surgery will be in Mexico City, about five hours away. They're all going to drive and stay with relatives until Girasol gets out of the hospital. The workers on my abuelo's ranch probably know more about the whole situation.

My dad lights a candle, and we both kneel down. I know I'm supposed to be praying, but I have a lot of feelings that I can't sort out. The fear. What if something bad happens to Girasol? The anger. Why did this have to happen to my sister? The hurt. Nobody cares what happens to me as much as they care about

Girasol. The confusion. I don't know what they expect me to do. The hope. Mostly, I hope everything goes back to normal.

On the way back from mass, my dad drops a bombshell on me. The International Surgical Group makes special travel arrangements for family members to be at Girasol's hospital during her surgery. My dad wants to know if I will take his place. He can't go—remember why? You know how they say you're between a rock and a hard place? Well, I'm there all right. I'm between an electric rock and a hard place with prickles. If I go, I'll miss soccer, let my team down, and maybe get stranded in Mexico for the rest of my life. If I stay, I'll let my family down, and my dad will think I don't care enough about my mom and Girasol.

"I don't know, Dad. There's school and soccer." I don't tell him that I'm also petrified of traveling all by myself, especially the flying part.

"Worry about yourself, Sandro."

So I do worry. All afternoon. While I clean Frankie's box.

"When is that nuisance going back to school?"

"We promised Girasol we'd wait."

I worry all through my homework.

"Mamá asks me about your tests. Are they good?"

"They'll probably send my results home sometime soon."

And I worry while I pick up and put my dirty clothes in the washing machine.

"Don't forget to put the load in the dryer while I'm at work."

The phone rings. It could be my coach. I'm excited but also sad. If our game is rescheduled during the week, my dad will be working. Then I remember I might not even be here for the game anyway if I go to be with Girasol. I can hear him talking and arguing, then he yells for me.

"It's Mamá."

I pick up the receiver. I listen and nod and listen and nod. "Okay, Mamá. Okay. I will. Te quiero."

When I hang up, my dad says, "I already know."

And it's settled. I'm not going to Mexico City. Mamá does not want me to travel alone. She has enough to worry about, doesn't she? Yes, we Zapotec men are strong and stubborn, but we wrap right around my mamá's finger.

•

I run into the house after school on Monday and listen to the answering machine. No message about soccer. One message from the business department of one of the hospitals. One message from Mr. Smalley. Wait, Principal Smalley?

"Please call me at your earliest convenience," his voice booms from the machine.

My stomach feels wobblier than a lopsided soccer ball. My nose has been squeaky clean. In fact, Mr. Smalley passed me on the way to the dumpster today and said, "Keep up the good work."

I decide to erase the messages. If it is important, Mr. Smalley will call back. I also decide to find out where to pick up my check for all this recycling I'm doing. Surprising my dad with the money in the next few days might soften any blows that are heading my way once he and Mr. Smalley talk. I call the recycling center and leave a nice message for the nice lady there, who doesn't answer the phone. As I'm replacing the receiver, I see Miguel's head bobbing outside my door.

"What?"

"Soccer."

"There was no message on my machine about a game rescheduled for today."

"Not the game. Practice. Remember?"

This is what happens when too many things are on a plate. Something falls off. I grab my gear and jump in his car, but in my rush I forget to put the rock by my door and hang my backpack on the hook in the closet. I think of it while we're zipping across town, and I cross my fingers and hope that Mrs. Arona keeps out.

Two hours later, I can see that crossing my fingers is a worthless superstition. Mrs. Arona's kids are on my porch with Frankie. Mrs. Arona yells at them in

Spanish, and they jump up, plopping Franklin down, and scurry back to their duplex.

"I'm sorry, Sandro. Your phone. Ringing and ringing. My meat burning on the stove." She throws up her hands.

Her kids don't go to Lincoln Elementary. They're too little. So at least they won't tell their teachers they know where Franklin's kidnapper lives. I hold open the door and Franklin walks into the house, not appearing too dazed from his fall. He looks okay, but I'm not an expert on shellshock. Steam rises from the meat and beans Mrs. Arona left on the counter, and my stomach growls. I see my backpack dumped out all over the floor. Those darn kids. Can't she keep an eye on them?

The phone rings. It's my dad. "Sandro, what's wrong with the answering machine? I'm calling and calling."

"I don't know." Once I look at it, I see I forgot to reset it.

"Listen. Girasol and Mamá left for Mexico City. I work tomorrow all day with Pablo roofing. Mamá will call. You must come from school right away and go nowhere."

"But Dad, what about—?"

"No empiezas."

CHAPTER 9

Extenuating Circumstances

D id you ever try to add just a little bit more soda to your cup and *sploosh*, it overflows? Did you ever blow one last puff into a balloon and *kapow*, it pops? I always know when to stop. But by the time I figure it out, it's too late.

Worry about yourself, Sandro, I remind myself almost every day, but Sandro the selfish brat doesn't pay attention. I'm standing here in line waiting for the bell to ring, wondering why I didn't see Miguel on the way to school. Then I remember he has a doctor's appointment. Shoot, I wanted to practice penalty shots with him at recess. And I also wanted to talk him into recycling for me today since my dad wants me to come right home.

As I stand there, I see Abiola come riding up on her bike. Who rides a bike to school in November anyway? I'm trying to mind my own business and not be mesmerized by the shininess of the bike. I see a new water bottle holder attached to the frame and a little saddlebag hanging from the back of the seat. And is that a compact air pump on the seat tube? If I keep recycling until I can grow a beard, maybe I will have enough money to add all those accessories to my new bike. *After paying for Girasol's surgery, of course,* reminds Sandro the hero.

After locking up her bike, Abiola walks right up to me. "Marta says you cough at me and hold your breath."

I give her my best what-are-you-talking-about face and shake my head. Boy, you have to give her credit. She sure knows how to attack a problem face-to-face.

Jazzy, who is standing in front of me, turns around. "Sandro, that is soooooo mean."

I give her a scowl. She's acting like she didn't cough and hold her breath, too. Where is Miguel when I need him to back me up?

Jazzy lets Abiola cut the line, and they start whispering and giggling, staring back at me every once and a while.

"No, he *didn't*. Oh, my gosh. That is *too* funny." Jazzy is talking super loud, so more girls are getting in on the conversation. I could use a winter hat right about now. Pulled down over my whole face.

Lorenzo is waiting by the coat hooks when I enter the school. "Did you really think Abiola's mom was kidnapping Miguel's sister? That's rich."

It takes me a minute to remember Marta and the umbrella incident from the other day. I feel hot embarrassment flood my face.

"No. I just didn't know what she was doing, that's all," I say.

So, are you visualizing like we talked about? Do you see what is happening to my life? Even the Avengers have bad days, but bad weeks? Bad months?

"Sandro?" Miss Hamilton is standing by my desk with her tablet. "Did you give that letter to your father?"

What should I say? I used to know what to do in these situations, but I'm losing my touch. You think I should say yes? Okay.

"Yes."

"He didn't respond. I asked for a response." Miss Hamilton is testy.

"Uh. He's real busy. I'll remind him."

She walks away, marking something in her grade book.

Abiola's desk is one row over and up. I hear her whisper, "Oooh. Is somebody in trouble?"

I stick out my tongue. I know, very childish. She raises her hand.

"Yes, Abiola," Miss Hamilton says.

"Mr. Smalley told me that if I feel threatened I should tell you right away," she says, glancing toward me.

Miss Hamilton stops collecting homework and checking it off on her tablet. She bends down close to Abiola. Next thing I know, I'm standing next to my chair, and Miss Hamilton is pulling my desk to the back wall.

"Sit. No more trouble out of you," she says, and then directs her attention to the rest of the class. "Let's get started on our morning assignments, shall we?"

I need a sinkhole to swallow up me and my problems. I need a time machine to take me back to that moment when everything started to go belly up. Help me out here. When did my life suddenly take a turn for the worse? Are you thinking what I'm thinking? I'm thinking of a cold-blooded, snaky-eyed, shell-packing stowaway—that's when it all started. Well, Franklin, mi casa no es su casa. That's over. You are back to Lincoln Elementary first chance I get.

Finally the morning is over, and our class lines up for recess and lunch. Miss Hamilton calls the rows to line up, but I'm not in a row, so I'm last in line. No one notices when I drag my feet and meander down to the back of the school. I'm not up for any more humiliation today. I don't even care that some sort of activity is happening near the climbing gym and that it's roped off with yellow tape.

It seems as though I'm a vortex of bad luck. All around me swirl calamities that are out of my control. And to top it all off, my dad is now in trouble for collecting scrap metal at a prohibited site. He also told me immigration security might be raiding the factory during the night shift, which means my dad could be in even deeper trouble.

Even the Aronas are sucked into my unlucky storm. A piece of the scrap metal fell out of my dad's truck when he came home in the middle of the night, and Mr. Arona ran over it in the morning on his way to work. *Blewie.* He didn't look too happy fussing with his tire iron and spare tire when I passed him on my way to school.

Suddenly, Mr. Arona's flat tire gives me an idea. I take a little tiny rock and creep along the ground right up to Abiola's shiny new bike. I put my shoulder next to her Road Star semi-slick tread tires and press the little rock down into her tire valve. A satisfied sigh of air rushes out from the front wheel. I only wish I was deflating Abiola, not her tires. Don't get any ideas from my stupidity, though, because that's what it is. Stupidity. Some alien is invading my good senses and nullifying my Zapotec power at the moment.

Yes, there are extenuating circumstances behind my bad behavior. Do you need some help with that word? It means to thin out, but I think of it this way. There are circumstances that should extend you—extenu— forgiveness for what ate your good sense—extenuate. Um, that's still confusing, isn't it? Basically, it just means there are reasons to explain why you made some bad choices.

Let's add up my extenuating circumstances, shall we? 1) My best friend skipped school for a doctor's appointment; 2) my mom abandoned me to take care of my sister during her open heart surgery; 3) my calendar art was stolen by the teacher from the Shall-We planet; and 4) a rat-faced tattletale told complete lies about me.

Remember, I always know when to stop *after* it's too late. People say hindsight is twenty-twenty. If I could do everything over, I would definitely wear glasses that give me perfect vision. And I'm not just saying that because Mr. Tomeski's shoe is two inches from my hand. When I look up, he grabs my jacket collar, yanking me to my feet.

"What do you think you're doing?" he growls.

Mr. Smalley asks the same question while staring me down in his office minutes later.

I want to say, "Nothing is as it appears. Look below the surface." But grown-ups should already know these things. I also want to say, "Do over." I want to say, "I'm sorry." Instead, I hear my alien invasion start talking.

Mr. Smalley listens as I make up stuff about how I was protecting the bike rack area from the little rocks that can cause accidents. He nods but doesn't answer. When he doesn't say anything, I keep talking, more and more, until I'm talking in circles, blabbing about nothing. And then it's as though he sprayed truth serum into the air because I get so confused I suddenly hear myself confessing to everything. Everything, that is, except stealing Franklin. That was *not* my fault. The Avengers would be ashamed of me.

Mr. Smalley asks Mrs. Lopez to call my dad and transfer the call to his office. I can hear the phone ring and ring, and then the answering machine comes on. Mr. Smalley leaves a serious sounding message. Mr. Smalley sends me out into the main office, where I'm directed to sit at a little desk in the corner

At noon, a fifth grader delivers my lunch before he sits down on the opposite side of the room at another little desk and eats his. I wonder what petty crime he committed today. Nobody bothers to give me any ketchup packets for my chicken nuggets or remembers that I do not like chocolate milk. But it doesn't really matter. I'm not hungry anyway.

The rest of the day, me and my schoolwork eavesdrop on the office hubbub. What a circus! I hear lots of confidential stuff and juicy gossip, so it's not too boring, but I do miss my friends. I also feel a gnawing termite nibbling on my stomach all day, but I can't figure out why.

By the end of the day, Mr. Smalley is quite upset that my dad didn't call him back or come to school to get me. He tries calling every number on my registration card. I conveniently forget my uncle's new cell phone number, and of course my mom is incommunicado.

"You tell your parents I need emergency contact information for them by tomorrow," he barks and then tells me I can head home.

I light out of his office faster than a speeding bullet and evade answering questions from the busybodies in my class as I collect my things and head out the front door. Tomorrow I'll pay for skipping recycling, but I'm anxious to follow my dad's instructions and get home right after school. Probably a good idea, don't you think? I already have enough adults mad at me.

Four messages are blinking on our answering machine. One from a hospital collecting money again. Three from Mr. Smalley. None from Mamá. I delete the three from Mr. Smalley. I'll just tell my dad what happened. It would be better coming from me, don't you think? I stand in the living room and wait. I sit and wait. I snack and wait. A watched pot never boils, and a watched phone never rings. When it finally does, I jump a mile.

"Hello."

"Sandro?"

"No messages, Papi."

"Chale! I need to know. Why doesn't she call?"

"I don't know, Papi. Maybe there's no signal in the hospital room, and she doesn't want to leave Girasol."

"Sí, sí. This is true. How was school, Mijo?"

Do you think it's a good idea to tell my dad that I have to do my homework in the office for the rest of the week? In-school suspension, they call it. The phone is not a very good conductor for that kind of information. And he's pretty worked up about Girasol. Wait, you say? Good call.

"School was good. They're doing some work on the playground."

After I hang up, the termite starts chomping all around the edges of my stomach again. I don't want to be too far from the phone, but I scoot down the hall, open my bedroom door, and yell, "Start packing, you turtle with a half-shell!" I feel a little better. Franklin is nosing around in his bark. "It's curtains for you, you cold-blooded creature." I kick the box, and Franklin pulls his head into his shell. The phone rings.

"Sandro? Oh, Sandro, Mijo, how are you? We miss you so much."

"How's Girasol?"

"Perfect. Already her color is better. She's asking for you. Here she is."

Me? My sister wants me? The liar. The bully. The selfish brat. "Girasol?"

"Doe-doe?"

"Sí, Girasol, it's me."

"I had an operation."

"I know. How do you feel?"

"I get vanilla ice cream."

"Good. That's good."

"Did you like my pictures?"

"Yep. Really good."

"Is Franklin okay?"

"Yep. Here he is." Then in my best Franklin impersonation I say, "Hello, Girasol. Thank you for saving me from Lincoln Elementary." Liar. Liar. Sandro the liar. I can hear old slowpoke scuffling around in his box, hopefully packing like I told him to.

Girasol giggles. "I want to take him back, Sandro. I had bad dreams, and Grandpa told me to make peace with Franklin."

I am dumbfounded, but I tell her, "Okay. When you come home." Wow. This is my little sister, one step away from a baby. The termites must have gotten to her, too. I guess Franklin will have a little longer to pack this things.

"Sandro?" says Mamá. "Sandro, I have to go. Tell Papi everything went better than expected. The doctor says two weeks before she can travel, and then we'll come home. Te quiero, Sandro." And the line goes dead.

Now I've got termites and butterflies in my stomach. It's a regular insecto-world in there.

"Two weeks," I tell Franklin as I clean out his box and give him fresh food and water. "Two weeks and the curse of Sandro will be lifted. Two weeks before my life is back to normal."

I sure do have a lot of problems to solve in two weeks. Let's not think about it, though, okay? Let's play some video games. Let's watch some TV. It might be my last night on earth once my dad finds out about Mr. Smalley's office, and I want to enjoy it.

CHAPTER 10

The Clean Sweep

It's truly amazing how much work I get done in the front office all week. Wednesday I wake up super early and complete the recycling before my office incarceration, so I'm tired right from the start. I have a hard time focusing with all the activity going on around me, but then I tell myself, *Worry about yourself, Sandro, and not about all the interesting problems in the office.* I knuckle down and do everything Miss Hamilton sends to me during the day. I write a full page in my journal and do the bonus math problems, which I usually never do. This prisoner reform system (aka in-school suspension) seems to be working. I'm a new and improved Sandro.

People say things happen for a reason. Maybe I was getting too comfortable in my full bathtub. Just floating along. But now that the water is leaking out, I'm turning on the faucets and paddling hard. And look at the results. I'm more organized and industrious. And, to use Mr. Smalley's word, philanthropic. Of course, it is only day two of solitary confinement but still.

Concentrating on reading is tougher, especially since our new novel is full of Greek myths. In the first one, Atlas, one of the Titans, loses the war against Zeus, and for his punishment he has to carry the world on his shoulders. Actually, not just the world but the whole celestial atmosphere, which I'm guessing is huge. I'm trying to do close reading to understand Atlas by making connections to the stories my dad tells about the Zapotecs. Strong intelligent warriors who designed whole civilizations.

On Thursday there's more to read and some response questions to answer, and I maintain my new work ethic. I even add a little research about the Zapotecs as I write my opinion essay. I should mention that my Zapotec dad still has no idea that his wannabe Zapotec son is in hot water. Our schedules are not so conducive to father-son heart-to-heart talks or, in my case, confessions.

Mr. Smalley leaves with his briefcase after the bell rings on Thursday afternoon. "If you get in contact with Sandro's father, tell him to call me this afternoon," he tells Mrs. Lopez.

The secretaries are starting to really enjoy my company, since I've been using my best win-them-over manners. They sure do laugh a lot. And they snack on goodies all day. By mid-morning, I finish all the new stuff Miss Hamilton assigns. Mrs. Lopez puts me to work on a paper-clipping project. I knock it out before you can say jackrabbit, and all the secretaries applaud me, making a big deal about my paper-clipping skills.

I don't think I'm supposed to leave the office during my in-school suspension, but they send me on a couple of errands anyway and reward me with a doughnut. Just before lunch, two parents bring Happy Meals for their kids, and I get to deliver them. I'd be lying if I said I didn't steal a french fry, but who can resist that smell? My lunch arrives in the office and a bunch more school-work. I stare at the pile of papers and books. Why do kids have to work this much?

Mr. Smalley comes back from his meeting after lunch, and the office climate gets more serious. Every once in a while, one of the office ladies gets something from the files near me and ruffles my hair. It makes me really miss my mom, and the butterflies in my stomach dance a little bit.

I haven't talked to Miguel for days. I don't even know if his doctor's appointment went okay. I don't even know if we have soccer practice after school. I don't even know if Abiola figured out who flattened her tires. If she knows, then the whole class knows. Cheese Whiz. I might have to ask for a school transfer. Can I do that? Maybe I should go live with my grandparents in Oaxaca and make a fresh start.

Before I leave for the day, Mr. Smalley asks me to join him for a chat. "Sandro, your parents have not responded to my phone calls. Tell them to call me tomorrow, or on Monday I will be forced to take action."

"Yes, sir." *Sir*, that's a nice touch, don't you think? But really I'm wondering what sort of action he can take. Out-of-school suspension? Make me scrub the floors?

"And Sandro, the Kahns are not going to press charges. They understand you may be having some trouble adjusting to your family's situation."

"Yes, sir." Well, I guess that means Abiola *does* know who sabotaged her bike. But this news makes me angry instead of relieved. Who told them about my family? It's none of their business. There are laws about privacy, aren't there?

"Next week you will follow procedures and not irritate your teacher or antagonize Abiola. Do you understand?"

Once again, Mr. Smalley is one-upping me on hard words. I assume antagonize means bother in a bad way.

"Yes, sir." But what about my persecutors? Do they have to follow procedures? Does Miss Hamilton have to stop harassing me? Does Abiola have to stop tormenting me?

I head out to take care of my recycling project; each bag I lug drains my strength. Me and Atlas. The weight of the world on our shoulders—our punishment for rebelling. I make the second trip into the lunchroom for more bags. If only I knew how much money I've earned for Girasol, I could end this punishment. I don't even care what Sandro the selfish brat wants anymore. New bikes are overrated, anyway.

This Saturday I will demand information from the recycling center driver. I need to know how to collect my checks. I lock the dumpster. It's not even January, and already I'm making my resolutions. 1) Demand to know how to get my money; 2) clean the house to surprise my mom; 3) be a better brother to Girasol; 4) never speak to Abiola again.

I heard that if you always do things the same way, it makes your brain soggy, so all week I've been walking home by different routes. I live eight blocks away from school, and I'm on variation four not counting Miguel's usual way. He's certain his way is faster. I try to explain to him that eight blocks is eight blocks, no matter if you go straight and turn once or turn eight times, but he can be quite pigheaded.

Anyway, on my route today I see some seedpods that are shaped like Christmas ornaments, little prickles poking out around the holes. Girasol loves Christmas. I could decorate her mirror with these. I pick up a few.

My dad already told me that Christmas will be thin this year (which is a nice way of saying I won't be getting many presents). I look down at the seedpods. The dry leaves near the pods are perfect five-pointed star shapes. I wish I knew this tree's name. Mamá loves plants. Maybe I could grow her a seedling for Christmas from one of these pods.

That's when I see a flash of something orange and red wedged under the muffler of a broken-down Ford pickup. I bend down and look closer, and I see the most beautiful sight I have ever seen. An Adidas Predator soccer ball. And it looks brand new.

At first I think my luck is changing and that this soccer ball is my reward for all the donkey doo-doo that has happened to me over the past few weeks. Then, while I'm lying under the truck with my face staring up at its greasy underbelly, I think, *No, this ball belongs to somebody. I will rescue it and return it and reverse the Sandro curse.*

It's not an easy task, but I use my inventor's skills to maneuver the ball around the axel case and sharp stuff, getting my hands full of black gunk and my shirt wet and muddy. By pressing down, I can almost push the ball out, but there's no way it will make it past the muffler pipe.

I just happen to have a paper clip from the paper-clipping project. Don't even accuse me of stealing, okay? It's one paper clip, and I found it on the ground. I wiggle my hand into my pocket, pull the clip out, and bend it, then poke it into the valve. Ironic, isn't it? Now I'm deflating something for a good reason. The ball flattens just enough, and I shimmy out from under the truck with it. As I emerge, I see two little legs standing on the curb, then a little brown face with dark eyes staring at me.

I hold the ball toward the little boy.

"Here you go, it's still okay. I just deflated it to get it unstuck."

"La-La," he yells and runs around the side of the apartment building. He says some other stuff I don't understand. He comes back with a compact air pump and hands it to me. I dig in my backpack for my air pump needle, which I always carry for the flat soccer balls at school. I show the boy how to screw it to the pump hose, and I hold the ball while he pumps. His teeth are so white when he smiles at me, and a spot under my ribs gets a little warm. He makes me miss Girasol.

The boy runs away again yelling, forgetting to give me the needle back. Oh well. I've got a whole bag of them. I feel pretty good about myself. But then I see a girl in soccer shorts and shin guards walking around the corner and hear her make a whooping sound. She yells, "Wait!" But I'm a secret Avenger, a masked Zapotec warrior, and I jog toward home without stopping, smiling inside.

The new-resolution me gets right to work cleaning the house to surprise my mom. Dad and I have sort of let things go a bit around the home. In fact, I'm getting downright lazy. Most nights I leave my dinner dishes in the sink so Mrs. Arona will have something to do when she comes over. And I hardly ever make my bed. What's the point if no one's around to see it?

First, I spray everything in the kitchen with some good smelling stuff I find under the counter, then I wipe it away in my best karate imitation. When I finish, the counter is streaky and a little sudsy, but boy it smells great.

I listen to the phone messages while I throw my soccer uniform in the dryer. I left it in the washer for a couple of days, and now it stinks. I hope the dryer fixes that. The first message is the hospital again. I wish I could ride my bike over there and hand them a wad of cash. *Here, this settles it. Now leave us alone.*

The second message is from Mrs. Arona. She's sorry that she won't be able to bring over dinner tonight. Her husband must work late to pay for a new car tire. She's bringing him dinner from La Estrella. I check the freezer for pizza and thankfully find one. Good. At least I won't go hungry.

The last message is from my soccer coach. Our game is Saturday at ten o'clock at the fields behind the high school. I give a fist pump. Yes!

Next, I tackle the piles on the floors so I can vacuum. I zoom around and throw everything into a laundry basket. The shoes by the door, the DVD boxes and remote controllers spread out on the rug, a TAICO work shirt that's on the back of a chair, some bags to recycle with flattened cereal boxes, and a stack of mail with lots of those coupon flyers in it—probably all junk mail. Holy guacamole, we sure are slobs. I will sort all the items in the laundry bin out later and put them away. Right now, it's clean-sweep time.

I don't know why moms seem to like cleaning so much. It's really boring. And vacuuming is the worst. I can't hear the TV or anything. After I vacuum the living room, I head into my bedroom and plow over the potato chips I spilled last night. The vacuum makes a really cool crunching noise. A great sound effect if you were giving a report on dinosaurs chewing bones or something.

Franklin's box smells a bit, too, so I decide to suck the bark out with the vacuum. Wow! Talk about sound effects. A little red light comes on the bottom of the vacuum, and the sucking stops. I smell burning rubber. I'm flipping the switches to troubleshoot the problem when I almost have a heart attack.

"Sandro."

"Ayyeee." I turn and there's Miguel. "You freaked me out!"

"You didn't answer the door, so I came in." His voice sounds crackly and lower than an old man's.

"What's wrong with your voice?"

"Bronchitis."

"Can you play soccer?"

"Maybe. Depends. I have medicine. Let's go. We are going to be late for practice."

I shovel some fresh bark into the box while Miguel says hello to Franklin, then I grab my soccer shoes out of the clean-sweep basket.

Once we're in the car, my stomach growls. Rats. I forgot to eat a snack. And with those termites in there chewing everything, I have lots of hungry holes. A vision comes to me of a pepperoni pizza oozing with cheese, and just for a second, I imagine ordering pizza from my favorite pizza place, Tommy Joe's. Who would know? I could secretly dispose of the box. I have twenty dollars in my drawer in a box marked BIKE SAVING. Better yet, you and I can split the pizza. Ten dollars each. What do you say?

Funny how soccer takes my mind off everything—even food. For an hour and a half I'm a normal kid with a wicked left foot. Cesar has trouble judging when to run up and get the ball and when to hang back and protect the goal, so we practice this move over and over again. Finally Coach puts Jared back in goal. This makes me uneasy about Saturday's line up. Will coach play the hand with me and Jared? Or the one with Noel and me? Or another hand altogether with me on the bench?

After practice, I bake the frozen pizza, using my self-control not to touch my bike savings. Papi calls and tells me he talked to Girasol and Mamá. They might come home sooner than two weeks. When I tell him there's soccer on Saturday he doesn't say anything. I know what he's thinking.

"It's okay, Papi. It's not the championship yet."

"I may have to work on Saturday."

I'd be lying if I said I wasn't sad, but it can't be helped. Making money to pay for Girasol is way more important than a silly soccer game. After devouring my pizza, I do my homework and take a shower. It's too late to take care of the laundry basket from the clean sweep. First thing in the morning, I will sort and put everything where it goes. I put away the worthless vacuum and step on something crunchy. I spilled Franklin's bark on my carpet. Well, tomorrow I'll sweep it up with the trusty old broom.

"Sandro?" It's Mrs. Arona. She must be in the kitchen.

"Sí."

"Sandro, why is the kitchen so slippery?"

"I cleaned."

"Show me what you use."

I pull the bottle from under the sink, and she tells me it is dish soap. It does not mention anything about dish soap. It reads DAWN ULTRA 3 in big bold letters on the front. She points at the little tiny words under the big bold words. Oh, yes, it does mention dishwashing liquid. Now who's gonna read those tiny little words? Come on, people. She hands me a wet cloth, and she and I wipe and rinse and wipe and rinse until my fingers are puckered up and raisin-ish.

I'm snuggled down deep in my puffy quilt, drifting off into soccer dreamland, where the fields are slippery with Dawn Ultra 3 and I'm slide tackling left and right when my door opens.

"Sandro?"

"Huh?"

"Where is the remote for the TV?"

"What?"

"The remote. For the TV."

"Oh. Uh. In the basket."

"What basket?"

"In the kitchen. The laundry basket."

She says a not very nice word in Spanish. "The basket is dumped into the garbage."

I sit up so quickly that I'm dizzy. "What?" And then I remember that I put the bag with recycled cereal boxes and the junk mail on top of the basket. Of course, that did make it look like garbage. But who takes other people's garbage out? Mrs. Arona, that's who.

Shizam. I shoot out of bed and stub my toe on Franklin's box. Here's the thing. We live in a duplex. And our duplex is part of a bunch of duplexes. And we all share a big green dumpster that sits in the alley. So my clean sweep is now in that big green dumpster. Cheese Whiz.

Mrs. Arona holds a flashlight and the back of a chair we brought out to the alley as I lean over the edge of the dumpster. The first thing that happens is I'm knocked senseless by the rotting refuse smell. My pizza dinner tries very hard to escape from my stomach. I pull my pajamas up over my nose and pray I don't fall in.

Oh man. Oh man. This is so gross. I'm touching nasty creepy slippery stuff. I think I see my dad's shoe. Yes. It's his shoe. Covered with something yellow. And this bit of blue material might be his shirt. By golly, it is. Yuck. Note to self—use two capfuls of laundry detergent when I wash the clothes this week.

By the time I'm done, we've filled the laundry basket up halfway. I found three shoes, my dad's work shirt, and the TV remote but not the DVD remote. The mail I recovered is wet and mushy, and I distinctly see an electric bill, so it wasn't all junk after all. The DVD boxes are kind of cracked and broken, and I can't remember what else to look for. My dad might have to come in the daylight to find the rest of our things. Wait. My dad? Holy cow. I'm in trouble now.

"No more cleaning for you," says Mrs. Arona.

I want to say, "No more throwing away garbage for you," but I can't speak. My teeth are chattering and not just from the cold. I'm horrified. I've lost count of all the reasons I'm in trouble. Do you have a spare bedroom? I'm not picky. I can sleep on the top bunk or the bottom. Put in a good word for me with your mom, okay?

I help Mrs. Arona wipe and rinse the items once we get inside. My dad's three shoes look semi-okay. The mail does not. I'm super glad my soccer shoes escaped the clean-sweep disaster.

While I'm taking my second shower of the day, I hear the TV go on, so I know the remote still works. By the time I get to bed it's late, late, late.

I dream I hear my dad talking to Mrs. Arona. "Such a disappointment. Our only son. He can no longer live in a Zapotec house." I'm driving away with an officer of some sort when I see Girasol arrive in a limousine. The last thing I see from the rear window is Girasol walking up the steps, my dad holding dozens of roses, and my mom overloaded with pink stuffed animals. Girasol turns and blows me a kiss.

"Sandro. Sandro. Shhh. Shhh."

I open my eyes and lift my head. My dad is sitting on my bed pushing my hair off my forehead.

"You're dreaming. It's okay now."

I sink back into my pillow. I wish I could tell him that my nightmare is not as bad as the daymare he's going to have when he wakes up.

CHAPTER 11

One Man Standing

There's nothing to tell about my last in-school suspension day. Mr. Smalley doesn't mention taking action with my dad. Maybe he was just trying to scare me.

Mrs. Lopez gives me my spelling test. She whispers, "You just missed one word."

"Which word?"

"Weight."

"No, I spelled it right. W-A-I-T."

"Not that 'wait.' It's the other 'weight.'"

"How am I supposed to know which one you meant? You have to give me a sentence using the word."

"Oh," she says and looks disappointed, as if she messed up her debut as a spelling tester.

"It's okay," I tell her. "I know how to spell both. W-E-I-G-H-T, as in 'You look amazing. Did you lose weight?'"

She laughs. "Okay. And you better W-A-I-T until you're older before you start flirting."

Finally the day is over. After taking care of the recycling, I walk home using one more different route. I do think it's good for your brain to vary your routine. I'm definitely noticing more things than I used to. And as I round the corner, I notice my dad's truck in our driveway. Whoopee! Maybe we can practice some soccer together if he has the afternoon off.

Then my super-charged brain has another thought. Maybe it's not good that he's home this early. What if he reinjured his back? What if he's in trouble at the TAICO factory? What if he bumped into his boss, Mr. Kahn, and mentioned that his son Sandro just happened to be a fourth grader at Lincoln Elementary? Did you ask your mom about me visiting for a while? I might need that invitation soon.

My dad is sitting at the kitchen table as I plow through the door. I see three letters spread flat out in front of him. His face is concrete hard. I freeze. It's not my dad that's in trouble. It's me.

"Sandro. Sit. Do you remember that I tell you worry about yourself?"

"Yes, sir."

"Don't smart talk me."

"Yes, Papi."

"Do you remember that I tell you, be the better man?"

"Yes, Papi."

I can see that the letters on the table all have my school logo at the top. One of them is stained with dumpster slop. Uh-oh.

He points at the first letter. "Did you erase any phone messages? Did you keep the mail from me? Why does your teacher say I did not respond?"

See what I mean about adults firing questions at you? "Uh . . . well . . . I might have left the letters in my backpack."

He holds out his hand. I dig in my backpack and retrieve the envelopes.

He rips them open, and his head sort of jerks back and forth. "Sandro. Your teacher wants me to give permission for a social worker to talk with you."

"Why?"

"You tell me."

I rack my super-charged brain that has suddenly gone back to soggy waffle brain. What is a social worker? Is that the person who takes you away from your parents? Or is that a caseworker? Maybe it's that nice lady with the curly black hair who talks to kids at school. It's hard to admit I don't know this stuff, but I need to know. "What's a social worker?"

"It's a person who works with kids with problems."

"Oh. But I don't have problems. There's a girl who doesn't like me. That's all."

"It says here you have trouble adjusting to fourth grade and need help with crisis management."

"I think they're exaggerating. It's just a misunderstanding."

"Not true. I have two letters from your principal. Vandalism. Bullying. Suspension."

"Oh." My mouth seems to be stuck in a circle shape.

"Sandro, I don't understand."

"This girl, Abiola, is ruining my life. She tattles and gets me in trouble."

"Sandro, are you worrying about yourself?"

I shake my head.

"Sandro, are you being the better man?"

My face gets hot. I'm ashamed.

"You have let the Zapote family down. You have let me down. But worst of all, you have let yourself down."

I feel pretty sorry for myself right about now. No one understands me. It's not all my fault. I'm being blamed for everything. I need my mom. A drop of water leaks from the corner of my eye. I bet even Atlas shed some tears when he picked up the world and put it on his shoulders.

"Now we must all worry about Sandro as well as Girasol? You are to stay in this house. Do not get into trouble." He points at the yucky mail I fished out of the dumpster and then at the laundry basket. I see he found his other shoe and the DVD remote.

"I'm going to substitute on the third shift tonight. Then I will go straight from work to Pablo's in the morning to help with the roofing. Mamá is not to worry about this. Do you understand?" He folds up the letters, puts them in his pocket, and exhales with a little growl as he gets up.

I understand perfectly. I understand that my dad will be gone all night working the graveyard shift and that I will be home listening to the spooky graveyard noises that come in the middle of the night. I understand that Mamá will not be on my side giving me sympathy and easing my punishment. I understand that I am grounded with no end in sight and that the biggest soccer game of my life is tomorrow.

Now think back with me. Did he actually say that I'm grounded? He could have meant that I have to stay in the house tonight—not stay in the house forever. The more I ponder this, the more I'm sure I'll be able to get away with soccer tomorrow and, of course, meet the recycling truck at school. Uncle Pablo and my dad will work from early morning to late afternoon. I'll straighten out the recycling situation, ride my bike to the high school, beat the pants off the opposing team, and be home before my dad returns from roofing with Pablo.

I'm sensing your concern. I agree. This might be a bad idea. But I've got to get the money, don't I? Won't my dad appreciate cold hard cash in light of my recent failures? And my team is counting on me. If I stay in the house and they lose, I will never forgive myself. My Zapotec honor is at stake, isn't it? Okay. Good idea. I'll sleep on it and see what the morning brings.

•

The morning finds me riding along the street with my light jacket over my soccer uniform. I splash a little of my dad's cologne on my jersey to offset the leftover smell of mildew. My water jug is full and hanging from my handlebars. Even on chilly days it's important to stay hydrated.

When I get to Lincoln Elementary, I lean my bike against the bike rack and unlock the dumpster. No sign of the recycling truck. Usually he's here by now, but of course, since I'm in a rush today, he's going to be late. Just my luck.

I walk around to the front of the building so I can watch for him to come down the main street. I see some big kids head over to the playground. It sort of looks like Black Hole Noel, but I'm too far away to recognize him. And anyway, Noel is probably still in bed, just waking up to the smell of a fantastic breakfast full of super energizing foods to keep him super charged for our big game. I can't wait to be in middle school. I'll be much cooler than Black Hole Noel. Middle school has a soccer team and art classes. And once I'm in that big school, chances are Abiola and I will never cross paths again. I hear the truck and run around the back to meet the driver.

"Hey," I say when he rolls down his window.

"Is it unlocked?"

"Yah. Hey," I say again.

But he is already pulling the truck up to the dumpster. The front forks lift the bin and the covers flap open, dumping all the bags into the back of the truck.

The driver leans out and hands me a yellow paper.

"Hey, I have a question."

"What?"

"Where do I take the receipts to get paid?"

"What?"

"You know. For all the loads. I've got the receipts, but I don't know where to cash them in."

The driver turns off the truck and jumps down from the cab. "What are you talking about? We've been paying you for each load. The check's sent out."

"I didn't get any checks."

"The school gets the checks. They're fixing the playground. I read about it in the newspaper."

I look over at the playground. Sure enough. Black stringy stuff that reminds me of a combination of

Franklin's bark and Jazzy's hair spreads out under a new slide apparatus.

"All right, then?" He swings back up, slams the door, and rattles off.

No. Not all right. All this work and nothing for Girasol. Nothing for me. Well, sure, she'll use the playground when she comes back to school. But I never agreed to that. Or did I? Is that what "nonprofit charitable organization" means? Cheese Whiz. I'm steamed. All those hours of lifting bags. Why didn't Mr. Smalley explain this to me? My heart feels like it's disintegrating. I can feel it falling away, piece by piece.

In the back of my mind, somehow, I know I deserve this. *This is your fault*, I tell Sandro the selfish brat. *You thought you could deceive the nonprofit charitable gods? You thought you could help yourself to the money your family needs? Now nobody named Zapote gets nothing. Way to go.*

Can't a guy get a break? I know it sounds wimpy, but I want to go home to my mamá. To a glass of milk. To a warm buñuelo. To her ruffling of my hair. I look around for my bike, but the rack is empty. I can't remember. Did I take the bike with me to the front of the school? I walk around and also look at the playground. But nothing. No bike anywhere.

Then it hits me. I know what happened. Oh, why didn't I lock up my bike like I always do? I try not to say the curse words I'm thinking. This is the worst day of my life. Did this happen because I disobeyed my dad? Did this happen because of Sandro the selfish brat?

Now I'm faced with another dilemma. Do I try to walk all the way to the high school? If I'm late, they won't even let me play. Do I walk home and skip the game altogether? If they lose because I'm not there, I will never forgive myself. I'm sick in my heart. What would a Zapotec warrior do? What would *you* do?

I take off running. After three blocks, I realize my water jug is on my handlebars, and I'm thirstier than a camel in the desert. If I keep running I might make it, but my legs will be toast by game time. After five blocks, I'm pretty sure this is a bad idea. I'm sweaty and chilly at the same time. If I get hypothermia and become unconscious, nobody will even know my name. People should always carry identification. Drivers have driver's licenses. Why don't walkers have walker's licenses? See, inventing is in my blood, even when I'm tired and cold and miserable.

Of course it will be tough to invent stuff from the confines of my four walls after my dad finds out I left home and lost my bike. My life is basically over. I'm a fourth-grade failure. Absolutely *nothing* I do turns out right. I'm the one who deserves to be sick. I'm a rotten, self-centered, greedy kid that nobody wants around. Thing is, I'd gladly take Girasol's place, but I didn't get the choice. Things *are* as bad as they appear. I can definitely visualize that.

After walk-running another ten blocks, I've lost all hope. The high school is nowhere in sight. My shoes are muddy. It's drizzling now. I'm about to turn around, put my tail between my legs, and crawl home to my prison if I can even find it, when I hear a car pull close to the curb. Probably some hecklers. I'm not going to look at them.

"Sandro. Sandro."

It's Abiola's voice. I glance over and see her leaning way out of the window yelling my name.

I'd rather see the creature from the black lagoon, or even my dad, than Abiola right now. The car stops, and the next thing I know, she's walking beside me. And in my exhaustion and depression, I imagine she is wearing soccer shorts and shin guards with a purple soccer shirt that reads RICHTON WARRIORS.

That's rich, isn't it? I'm supposed to be a warrior, but she's wearing the shirt.

"Sandro, what is wrong? Where are you going?"

"It's none of your business."

"Thank you for finding my ball."

Her ball? I'm stumped for a minute. Then I remember the truck and the ball and the little boy. And the girl. Oh man. This is unbelievable. The Masked Avenger does a good deed to end the Sandro curse, and it benefits his enemy. I should be on a talk show— the kid with the worst luck.

She doesn't say anything for a minute. Then she asks again, "Where are you going?"

"I have a game. At the high school."

"Well, that is where we are going. We will drive you."

You may think I'm a pushover. And maybe I am, but remember, if it were up to you, I'd still be sitting in the house. So I follow Abiola to her car. The cute little boy who helped me pump up the soccer ball is in a booster seat. And now I see the resemblance. Abiola slides into the middle seat and kisses him on his forehead. I shut the door and squish my body close to the door handle so my knee is not touching Abiola's.

"La-La." Her little brother smiles at me, and suddenly I miss Girasol again. Then he says something I can't understand and pats Abiola's cheek.

"This is my brother, Amir. He says you helped him fix my ball."

"Does he speak English?"

"He's learning. He also says you smell."

From the driver's seat, Abiola's mom says a torrent of words with harsh edges to them.

Abiola leans forward and says, "Okay, Ammi. Maaf karna." To me she says, "Sorry. But you do. And this is my mom, Mrs. Kahn."

"Hello, Sandro. I have heard many things."

So there it is. I'm a captive in a car with my enemy *and* I smell. (For your information, if you leave your soccer uniform in the washer too long, the dryer doesn't get rid of the stench. Then, if you get sweaty and wet, the odor amplifies into a dead, rotting fish smell that no amount of your dad's cologne can conceal.)

Mrs. Kahn looks at me in the rearview mirror. "Do you also play soccer?"

She talks the same as Abiola except with an accent. I almost say, "Yah," but she's so proper I find myself saying, "Yes, Mrs. Kahn."

"It is a good sport, would you agree?"

"Oh yes. It is."

"Abiola very much enjoys soccer."

Then I realize I wasn't imagining Abiola wearing soccer gear. She actually plays soccer. Real soccer? On a team? Well, that would explain the soccer uniform, wouldn't it? And her insanely perfect soccer socks pulled up and folded over meticulously. This is incredible. I've never seen any girls on our soccer fields. Or maybe I just didn't pay attention before. "What team are you on?" I ask her.

"The Warriors. It is a premier league. We are going to California for an invitational tournament in December."

Good golly. Her team must be good. And now I remember her journal page. *Especially for my favorite game.* "I've never seen your team on the fields," I say.

"Oh, we usually play on Sundays. Home games are at the high school, but the away games are in different cities."

"What makes you walk today, Sandro?" Mrs. Kahn's eyes peer into my soul from the rearview mirror. Her hijab scarf—or whatever it's called—is under her chin.

I explain about the recycling project and about my stolen bike.

"Oh my. This should not be so. A good dog deserves a good bone."

I puzzle over this phrase a bit. I think it means hard work should be rewarded.

"And this money? You want to buy a new bike, yes?" she continues.

Who told her that? Abiola? And how did she know? Probably that no-good Miguel. I'm about to say yes because I hate talking about Girasol and her surgery and my family's problems. I hate people feeling sorry for me and my family. The termites in my stomach come alive and go crazy, but I'm tired and my guard is down.

I tell Mrs. Kahn everything from the very beginning. My mouth is running faster than an overflowing brook. And you know what? She is a very good listener. Her questions pull the stones from my babbling water to make it flow smoother. She asks a lot of questions about Girasol's sickness and operation, and I'm not sure I get it all right, but it feels good to let it all out finally.

I finish talking, and the termites are calmer. When I look out the window, I see that we are at the high school. Teams are everywhere. I almost don't want to get out of the car, I feel so peaceful. Mrs. Kahn is not at all how I imagined. Nothing is as it appears. I guess I know this, but I easily forget sometimes.

"I am sorry to hear of your troubles. It seems you have not eaten the soup but have burned your mouth. However, this is life's journey. Often difficult. A passenger is responsible for his own luggage."

My mind rolls this around. Hot soup is good, but it burns your mouth. I got burned by the recycling place and Mr. Smalley, but I never tasted the soup, which means I never got the money for my work. Aha. And luggage is something to carry. Burdens. Problems. Troubles. I have to solve those myself.

Abiola says something to her mom in another language and then tells me, "I'm coming with you to find your team."

I feel so weak and astounded by these new revelations that I can't bring myself to stop her from joining me.

"Adiós, Amir." He giggles and gives me his big smile. I can't wait to see Girasol smile like that again.

"How will you return to home, Sandro?" Mrs. Kahn asks.

This is a good question. I forget about my truth resolution for a minute and tell a little lie. "My dad's coming late to the game."

"This is good. If not, we will be at field nine for Abiola's makeup game. I'm glad to meet you. Abiola will always be happy to help you. One man standing is always alone, but two equals eleven."

It will be a cold day on the equator before I ask Abiola to help me. I'm already perturbed that she is volunteering to help me right now. But I tell Mrs. Kahn, "Thank you very much."

Abiola talks a mile a minute as we head out to find my team. Blah. Blah. Blah. I half listen while we walk. My mind is full of questions. What if there's a shortage of Zapotecs to stand with me to make eleven? I sure do feel alone, and my "luggage" is weighing me down.

"And that's why she goes to all the tournaments."

Whoops. I wasn't listening. "Why?"

"I just told you. My mom is almost a doctor in Pakistan. So she goes to the tournaments in case somebody gets hurt."

"Almost?"

"Do you not listen? She left Pakistan before she finished her studies. Maybe she will complete them when my brother goes to school. The system is complicated, she says."

I sigh. Everything is complicated. It's complicated for my dad, too. He trained for one job but is trapped doing another.

My dad, who reminds me of the man standing on the sidelines of field four. My dad, who looks just like the man now standing in front of me on the sidelines of field four. My dad? Oh boy. Abiola sees me stop dead as though I've come face to face with that rattlesnake, again. I've got to give it to her for perception. She gives me a half wave and skedaddles off to field nine. And why don't you take a clue from Abiola? Close the book. I need a little privacy.

CHAPTER 12

A Good Dog Deserves a Good Bone

You know how people say, "To make a long story short?" Well, here's the short version of the long story of what happened after you left me at field four with my dad standing in front of me. I'm in trouble. Apparently you and I were both wrong. "Stay in the house" meant stay in the house *all day Friday and Saturday*. Now I'm in the "less" department. Soccer-less. Bike-less. Moneyless. Friendless. Motherless. Hopeless.

I'm sitting on my bed. I'm reading my favorite book, *James and the Giant Peach*. It's about a boy who escapes from his horrible life by moving into a giant peach. Since I don't have a peach, I'm still considering moving to Oaxaca. I wish I wasn't so good at visualizing. *Flash*—I see my coach's face as my dad and I walk away from the field. *Flash*—I see Abiola turn and watch my dad grab the back of my jersey and propel me toward his truck. *Flash*—I see my dad's stone jaw as we drive home.

I don't know what's worse. Losing my bike. Losing the money from recycling. Losing the chance to help my team win. Or losing my dad's trust.

"When I need you to be more dependable than ever, you are irresponsible, deceitful, and reckless. Do my words mean nothing?"

At least he didn't force me to say I'm sorry. That was hours ago. I'm starving, and Franklin's food isn't very appetizing. My door opens.

"Mamá wants to talk to you," my dad says, dropping the phone receiver into my hand.

"Sandro? Pobrecito."

She tells me that she and Girasol will be home the weekend after Thanksgiving. She says that Girasol misses me. She says that she's sorry about my bike. She tells me, "Listen to Papi, Mijo. He's got too many worries."

Have you ever swallowed a big wad of gum that sort of sticks in your throat while going down? That's the lump I have in my throat after I hang up. My dad calls me to the kitchen and places bowls of soup on the table. I devour mine. He refills the bowl three times without saying a word. I may have to stop writing my life story. It looks grim. Nobody wants to read about a guy who's grounded to his bedroom for life, do they?

•

On Monday as I'm walking to school, I'm betting myself that Abiola has told everyone about my weekend misadventures. I see Miguel standing in line. He and Marta are in a morning carpool with their neighbors now that the weather is chilly. The lucky ducks.

"We lost," he says when I walk up next to him.

"I'm sorry. My dad—"

"Nothing you could do. Four to zero."

"Whoa. Really?"

"One crazy big player. Everyone think he's too old to be on the team."

"Cheese Whiz."

"Next year."

Abiola gets in line behind us. She doesn't say anything to me. *Be the better man, Sandro,* I tell myself. So I turn around and nod at her.

"Here," she says and hands me an envelope. "From my mom." I quickly stuff it in my pocket. My face gets a little hot, but I maintain my resolve. "Did you win your game?"

"Yes. One to zero. Close match."

I tell Miguel, "She plays soccer. Premier team." Abiola squints her eyes at me, searching my face, then her whole body straightens, and she smiles.

Miguel appears to have swallowed a bug and sputters before he chokes out, "Oh." Then he kicks the side of my shoe.

Obviously, I'm much more mature than Miguel.

"When's your tournament?" I ask Abiola.

"Next week. Have you ever been to California?" Her face has an eager gleam that I've never seen before.

"My mom was born there, but she moved to Mexico when she was young. Have you ever been to Mexico?"

Abiola smiles bigger in the same way her little brother does. "No. Have you ever been to Pakistan?"

We both laugh. Miguel scowls.

Once we are allowed into the building, I hang up my jacket and start into class when I remember the envelope. What could it be? I rip it open. The TAICO letterhead jumps out at me. It's a letter from Mrs. Kahn with beautiful loopy writing the same as Abiola's, which I'm pretty good at forging now.

I am letting you know I have started an online donation website for your family. It is confidential and secure. Donations are made anonymously.

Wait a minute. We've been forgetting your vocabulary in my boatload of troubles. That word anonymously is tricky to say and spell. I think of it this way: not *any*one will know, not even a *mouse*. Do you see parts of the words *any* and *mouse* hiding in *anonymous*ly? Okay, back to the letter.

The funds will come to your family from Lincoln School, so they will be easy to access. Please tell your father this was done for our family in our time of trouble, and there is no shame in it. My heart was heavy for you as I remembered my days of grief when we moved here. People must have opportunities to renew themselves with service. The website address is here with the information. Remember, after the rain comes fair weather.

I reread the letter three times and then run to get in my seat before the tardy bell rings. My mind is whirling. My dad will kill me. Again. But this isn't charity, is it? Nobody knows about it except for those at Lincoln School. Maybe Mrs. Lopez or the social worker are the ones who know. But doesn't my dad have to agree to this or something? And what troubles did the Khans have? Abiola never talked about any troubles, or did she?

I don't have time to worry about it. Miss Hamilton writes our assignments on the board with a reminder that she'll be selecting our best work to show our parents at conferences this week.

Well, if it doesn't rain, it pours. How are my grades, anyway? I decide to take the bull by the horns. When it's my turn for reading group, I zip over fast so I can sit next to Miss Hamilton and her grade book. From my peripheral vision, I find my name and scan across. Reading grades. Mostly B and C letters with a couple of Xs. Hmmmm. Those Xs are missing assignments.

"Am I missing any assignments for reading?" I ask.

"Just class participation and your response journal. When you aren't in class, I can't give you a grade."

"Can I make it up?"

"I've never done that before."

"I could write responses for the books I missed."

"You don't have much time. Grades are due next week."

"Could my parent-teacher conference be the week after?"

She passes out the books and some sticky notes. "Let's get started, shall we?"

"Could it? My mom really wants to come."

"We'll see, Sandro. Let's look at the table of contents, shall we?"

"My dad can't make it this week."

"I said, we'll see." Her words boom out. Prison doors slamming (not that I've actually heard prison doors, but I can imagine what they might sound like).

I'm on the verge of crying. If my mom comes home to one more disappointment from her son Sandro . . .

I bite my lip and try to make my dad's stone jaw face. I do my best to participate and respond. I'm about to walk back to my seat to get ready for recess when Miss Hamilton hands me three books.

"I think you missed writing responses to these three."

A good dog deserves a good bone. I put the three books in my desk and line up for recess.

Mr. Smalley intercepts me at the foot of the steps leading to the playground. "Congratulations, Sandro. Your recycling project is being recognized by the Board of Education. Come to my office for your award."

"Huh?"

"You and your parents will be invited to a board meeting. All the recipients will be presented with a plaque."

"A plaque?"

"I called an emergency meeting this morning. I was not aware that you orchestrated this project single-handedly."

Not aware? Didn't I meet with him and explain the whole thing to him? And why is he suddenly aware now? I think about my conversation with Mrs. Kahn.

He continues, "From now on, each classroom will have the responsibility of handling the recycling for a month. We will consider that your classroom has fulfilled its obligation thanks to your dedication."

I see Abiola in her polar bear hat standing alone by the edge of the playground. My buddies are streaking down the field after my favorite round black-and-white sphere. A huge weight lifts right off my shoulders.

I'm done with recycling duty? Hooray! But I actually feel kind of empty without the weight. Kind of unimportant. Like I might just float away and disappear. I wonder if Zeus ever offered to take the world off of Atlas's shoulders. "No, no, that's okay Zeus. I like the world on my shoulders. It makes me indispensable." Hmmm. That may be why Atlas still carries the world around.

Mr. Smalley is still talking, but I only hear the very end of what he's saying. "Very philanthropic, indeed." He shakes my hand and goes back into the school.

Before I know it, I find myself standing next to Abiola.

"Want to play soccer with us?" I ask her. Honestly, I'm not myself these days. Or maybe it's the polar bear hat. I really like polar bears.

"I can't."

"Why?"

"You won't let me."

Somebody signals me to join in the game. I tell myself, *Be the better man, Sandro*. I nod my head to Abiola. "Go on. Take my spot."

I can actually feel a tremor of disbelief rock the grass. My rule is: We do not allow girls to play. Never have. Never will.

Until today.

Rafe yells out, "Whaddya doing, Sandro?"

I almost yell, "Things are not as they appear!" Instead, I yell, "She can have my spot!"

Rafe stalks off the field as Abiola pulls off her polar bear hat and sprints onto the field.

Miguel passes the ball to Abiola. "Come on, Sandro."

So I take Rafe's place. Abiola blows by me with some fancy footwork. What's that noise? She's humming. A humming soccer player? Impossible. I'm already out of breath as I race to catch up and prevent the goal. Recess is over before anyone scores.

Miguel sidles up beside me as we walk in. "She's good."

"Yah, she is." And the truth is, she's better than Rafe and maybe even better than me.

•

I hurry home with Miguel and Marta since my recycling duty is officially over. Thanksgiving is three days away. I'm not looking forward to four days off school in the company of Franklin and my four walls, just waiting for Mamá and Girasol to return. As we walk, the tree branches clatter in the wind and random snowflakes flutter about. I really need to find my hat.

Once home, I open the big manila envelope that Mr. Smalley gave to me at the end of the school day. That's what those brown important envelopes are called. Not vanilla. Not salmonella. Manila. I read the certificate signed by Mr. Smalley, and I'm about to throw away the big envelope when something else falls out to the floor. It's a check from Lincoln School. Does it say $1,000? I pick it up and look more closely. No, silly Sandro. Things are not as they appear. PAY TO THE ORDER OF SANDRO ZAPOTE, $10.00.

While I'm in my room, I make a list of everything I can buy for ten dollars. And just so you know, I'm not saving one penny of it. So there. The list isn't very long because ten dollars isn't very much. Then I remember about the three books for my missing response homework and get started. The only time I leave my room that night is to grab dinner, use the bathroom, and answer the phone. It's my dad.

"Is the homework completed? Did Mamá call? What did you eat? Are you in your room?"

It's the inquisition. And I deserve it. I tell my dad about the certificate.

"Good. That's good."

"And Miss Hamilton is going to have my conference next week." That's not a lie, is it, even though she didn't totally agree to push it back?

"What conference?"

"The usual parent-teacher conference. Mamá will be home then, right?"

"Sí. That's good. Mamá will go."

"Also, Papi, there's a thing they started for Girasol. It's on the table."

"Mande."

"It's hard to explain." I pull out my ace card. "Mamá will be happy, though." This makes him calm down.

My dad must have warned Mrs. Arona that I am grounded because she comes over with her tablet and a magazine. I feel sad she'll miss her TV novellas on account of me being in trouble (my dad removed the TV and locked it in his bedroom). Then I have an idea.

"Mrs. Arona?"

"Sí, Sandro."

"I need an Internet connection for one little bit of homework. Do you think I could use your tablet?"

"Your dad tell me no games. No TV." She shakes her finger at me.

"No, no. This is homework. Ten minutes maybe."

Boy, I wish I had a tablet. They're so fast. The website Mrs. Kahn wrote down jumps onto the screen. I type in Girasol's name, and up pops her school picture with a paragraph about her disease. I notice that more than three hundred people have visited the site and that the goal for the money is half met. Whatever that means. I scroll up and down to find out. Whoa! The goal is set at $7,500. The bar is filled in up to $3,450. Does that mean what I think it means? This is amazing. I start reading some of the comments people have left:

My daughter was the same age as your daughter when she had the surgery. Today she is ten years old and healthy. Good luck. Anonymous
   Girasol is in my son's class. We are praying for you. Anonymous
   We hope this small donation will help your family. We are blessed to be a part of a community that cares about each other. Anonymous

I feel Mrs. Arona standing behind me. I quickly click out and jot down the information on the letter from Mrs. Kahn. I carefully cut off the top part that says TAICO, hoping my dad doesn't notice the little jagged part on the right edge. I fold it up and write DAD on the front, and then to be funny I write, TO MR. LISANDRO ZAPOTE FROM MR. SANDRO ZAPOTE. I crack myself up.

I'm drifting off to sleep when I decide to spend my ten dollars at Mr. Chin's Antique and Resale Shop. He's got lots of cool stuff at good prices. I will buy the first thing that catches my eye. I deserve a reward. And if there's any money left, I'll buy something for Girasol, too.

•

Thanksgiving is strange without my mom and Girasol. We go to my uncle's for dinner. My cousins are all little, so once I'm done playing horsie and tickle-tackle and hide-and-seek, I'm exhausted and escape to the back porch. I can see my breath, and it makes me think of Christmas. I don't even care about presents, though. Just to have my family home will be good enough. I watch my aunt and uncle bustling around the kitchen through the window while my dad leans on the counter. I bet he feels strange, too, being at my mom's brother's house without my mom.

In my pocket is my new gadget from Mr. Chin's. I'm still officially grounded, but while my dad did the grocery shopping, he let me go spend my ten dollars. He didn't say much about my certificate because he was stewing about the online donation website. I did my best to explain about one and eleven, but he said my math was wrong.

"One and one equals two. That's you and me. This is not somebody else's problem," he said. But he folded the paper up and put it in his pocket. In the break room at work, they have a computer with Wi-Fi. He'll check. I know he will. Then he can tell Mamá, and she will cry and be so happy.

I click open my new gadget. I love the way it shoots out of its case. When you shop at Mr. Chin's, you have to keep your money in your hand so he knows you're a paying customer. I made sure to flash my ten dollars when I asked him to show me the stuff in the case behind the counter. The minute he opened the glass door, it was the first thing I saw.

The slick pearly white handle has a shiny silver click button right in the middle. There's a stripe of turquoise around the top and the bottom. My grandpa has a shiny silver belt buckle that has the same pearly white in an oval with a turquoise stripe around it. In the middle of the oval on his belt is a silver longhorn steer.

Of course, I know his is made of real pearl or bone or something and mine is plastic. But what do you expect for less than ten dollars? The point is, when Mr. Chin opened the case and I saw something that reminded me of my grandpa, I knew I was meant to buy it. And I had enough left over for a puppy puzzle for Girasol. I tried to make sure all the pieces of the puzzle were in the box, but Mr. Chin said, "First you pay, then you play." Funny guy, huh?

Click. Click. Now you see it. Now you don't. I'm bringing it to school Monday for the shock and awe effect. Miguel will love it, don't you think?

CHAPTER 13

Visualize It, and It Will Be

My dad and I drive to the airport. Butterflies collide in my stomach. We wait at the end of a long hall. Some people have signs with names on them. Too bad I didn't think of that. I still have poster board left from my recycling campaign. I could write ZAPOTE in big capital letters and stretch the Z out like the Z in Zorro. No, maybe I could write GIRASOL and use the stick of the L for the stem of a sunflower. Did I ever tell you that Girasol means sunflower? I think I forgot to mention that.

And while I'm making signs in my mind, I see a little pink suitcase rolling along behind my very own sunflower sister. Girasol! I wave frantically and embarrassingly to get her attention just in case she's forgotten what her famous big brother looks like. She smiles and stops to wave back at me and almost causes a traffic jam. The second she and Mamá pass the security officer at the end of the ramp, my dad takes off and scoops up Girasol.

Then Mamá grabs me and squeezes so tight I almost suffocate. When my dad puts Girasol down, I start to hug her, but then I'm afraid. She's a shadow of herself. Thin and weak.

"Look, Sandro," she says and opens her mouth. "I lost a tooth."

She looks adorable with that little gap in her mouth.

"Did the tooth fairy come?" I ask her.

She places a tiny bag in my hand. "No, I saved it for you. You can put it under your pillow. Mamá says you worked very hard to help me."

My mom and dad are both watching me and Girasol. I know it's silly, but there's so much love right here, right now, it feels warm all around us.

•

Girasol falls asleep on the way home but perks up when she sees Franklin resting comfortably next to her bed in his nice clean box. I learned my lesson about vacuum cleaners and dumped the old wood chips in the garbage this time.

After dinner, Mamá puts Girasol to bed, and then the three of us sit in the living room listening to her tell stories about the surgery and my abuelos. We're all tired, and my dad's chin starts to dip to his chest just as Girasol screams. We all rush down the hall.

"You took it, Sandro. Give it back. Give it back now!" Her fists are clenched, and her face is pinched together.

Nobody else knows what she's talking about, but I do. I think I might have forgotten to mention to you that I borrowed her TV. Oh, don't lecture me. You would have done the same thing if you were all alone and grounded. When I come back into her room carrying her TV, my mom pats Girasol's hand and shushes her. My dad stares at me, shaking his head, disbelieving the depths to which I've sunk. Oh boy. More trouble.

I look at the clock on my bedside table. Ten o'clock. Sunday night. I can't get to sleep. I have a big day tomorrow. Girasol and I are restoring Franklin to his original habitat. I just don't know how we should do it. Sneak him in hidden in a backpack? Lie and say we found him by the side of the road? Be honest and claim we had a mental breakdown and thought he was our long lost relative? *Visualize it, and it will be.*

I'm thinking about the way the day went. My heart is riding a skateboard on a half-pipe—up, then down, then up again. It's great to have my sister and Mamá home, but Girasol sure gets a lot of attention. And she's still not back to normal. Mamá isn't, either. I guess my dad and I got used to being on our own. No more piling our plates in the sink. No more dumping our stuff by the back door. No more eating in front of the TV. And it's only been one day.

The door opens. Mamá pokes her head in.

"Sleeping?"

"No."

She comes in and sits on the edge of my bed. Cheese Whiz, it's been a long time. She ruffles my hair.

"Thank you, Sandro, for taking care of Papi. I know it was hard for you."

"It's okay."

"What happened at school, Mijito?"

"I didn't get along with one of the girls, that's all."

"What happened?"

I tell my mom a few of the details. A very few. Moms don't need to know everything.

She thinks for a while then says, "Why did she do those mean things to you?"

"I don't know. She wants attention, I guess."

"Maybe she's jealous of you."

"Me?"

"I would be jealous of you."

I laugh. And then I feel a little better.

"And this is the girl whose mother started the donations for Girasol?"

"Yes." Even my mom wants to rub it in that I might have been wrong about Abiola and her family. I want to say, "Things are not as they appear," but she won't get it. She's never seen *The Avengers*. I also want to say I'm sorry, but I don't.

It's uncomfortably quiet. Finally my mom says, "People have many faces, Sandro. Even our enemies. Sometimes the face of your enemy hides the heart of a friend."

This is something I imagine the Avengers might say, too. It makes sense. It's like "Don't judge a book by its cover." Of course, not all enemies have friendly hearts. I start thinking about all the bad guys I've seen in movies. Jabba the Hutt? No heart there. The Joker? Ruthless. Darth Vader? His heart didn't come out until just before he died. Hmmm.

"Sandro? Are you listening? Tomorrow I have your parent-teacher conference. I hope Papi can come for translating this big misunderstanding with your teacher. I want her to know it's not all your fault."

I'm alert now. I definitely don't want my dad to go. And the last thing a guy needs is his mom fighting his battles. "No, Mamá, don't do that. It's okay. Everything's okay now."

"And the principal?"

"I'm telling you. It's okay now."

"Well, I'm going to the office anyway to thank everyone and also to thank this girl's mother."

"It's confidential, Mamá. Anonymous. She doesn't want anyone to know."

"We can still thank her. This was a great thing she did for us."

She walks to the door. "Go to sleep, Mijo. Tomorrow you will be a better man."

After she leaves, I think of a thousand things I should have said. A good dog deserves a bone. I'm already a better man. I can carry my own luggage. One and one equals eleven. Nothing is as it appears. Visualize it, and it *might* be. But my last thought before I fall asleep is, *Worry about yourself, Sandro.*

•

Franklin is content in Girasol's pink backpack as we head to the office. I've taken a vow to tell the truth from now on, starting today. Really. I have. We march right up to the office counter, and Mrs. Lopez beams at me.

"What a pleasant surprise, Sandro. Is this your sister?"

I introduce Girasol, who acts shy all of a sudden. I coach her. "Girasol, tell them what happened." By this time, all the office ladies are up at the counter.

Girasol just looks at me. Unbelievable. I try again. "Tell them about Franklin."

Girasol shakes her head. Do *you* have a little sister? I'm not taking the blame for this. She better fess up and right now. Thank goodness Mrs. Lopez comes around the counter and bends down next to Girasol.

"Oooh. I love pink, too. Look at your cute shoes. Did you get those shoes on your trip?"

Girasol nods. I didn't even notice she got new shoes. I store this information away for future parent negotiations next time I want new shoes.

"Are you going to visit your class today? They sure missed you."

"She's going to visit today and then start again after winter break," I explain. I'm very knowledgeable on this subject, since I overheard my mom and dad arguing about it. If Girasol stays home, my mom can't work. If my mom can't work, they can't pay the bills. But if Girasol goes to school all day, she'll get too tired. If she gets too tired, she won't get better. Round and round.

Girasol pipes up, "I get tired."

"Oh, my. So do we. Can we all come and rest at your house?"

Girasol smiles. She opens her backpack. Franklin pokes his head out.

Mrs. Lopez jumps back a bit then recovers and acts all excited. "You found Franklin. Look everybody— Franklin's back."

I start to open my mouth to explain everything. I've taken a truth vow, remember? And I'm prepared to say I'm sorry. But Mrs. Lopez puts her finger to her lips and shakes her head. She gently pulls Franklin out of Girasol's backpack and walks off.

"You both better get to class. The bell is going to ring," the nurse says as she walks past us and out the office door. "Oh, and Girasol, welcome back."

I grab Girasol's hand and steer her out of the office.

•

During the morning announcements, Mr. Smalley says, "I hope everyone had a nice Thanksgiving. Today is an exciting day. Two of our friends are back at Lincoln Elementary. Welcome back Girasol Zapote. Kindergarten missed you. And our reptilian friend, Franklin, has come out of a short hibernation. Be sure to stop by and say hello. Lunch today is chicken nuggets or chef's salad. Mr. Wesley's fifth grade class is on recycling duty this week. We will have indoor recess due to inclement weather. Have a great day."

Miguel turns toward me, but I ignore him, not sure I can keep a straight face. See what happens when you carry your own luggage? Sometimes somebody comes along and carries it for you. I should make a little something for my office friends. Maybe my mom will help me.

When Miss Hamilton starts with our reading groups, I wander over to the pencil sharpener. But along the way, I pull my new gadget out of my pocket and show it off to a couple of my friends. In a short minute, there are a few of us at the pencil sharpener, but we're not sharpening pencils.

"Sandro, sit down," Miss Hamilton says above our giggles.

I sit. But a few minutes later, Jaylen asks me to show him my new gadget, and I oblige. We line up for art, and on the way, Lorenzo asks if he can see it. I knew this would be a big hit. It pops open like those umbrellas with a button, but it's small enough to fit in my pocket. We're still messing around when Mrs. Abernathy asks us to quiet down.

"I'm so excited to announce that for the first time one of our students has been chosen to represent the American Heart Association's postage stamp." She unrolls a poster and sticks it to the board with magnets. It's a giant-sized poster of a postage stamp with the words AMERICAN HEART ASSOCIATION down the side. The picture is of a heart with all the parts detailed and little speech bubbles.

Wait a minute.

That's *my* drawing.

My calendar page.

What in the world is happening?

Mrs. Abernathy continues. "Come on up, Sandro."

I'm dazed. Where did the American Heart Association get my drawing?

Mrs. Abernathy hands me a big envelope. It's the same size as the manila ones, but it's white. Then she hands me a certificate already in a frame. One of the real stamps is stuck to the middle, and it's dedicated to me. Cheese Whiz, this is cool.

"Congratulations, Sandro." She claps and so does everybody else. I see Mr. Smalley and my mom at the back of the room. Did they tell my mom about this award ceremony when she came for her parent-teacher conference? Is my mom crying? Holy guacamole. Don't cry, Mom.

"Open the envelope, Sandro," says Mrs. Abernathy.

I put the plaque on the ledge of the white board and tear open the flap. I pull out a letter and start to read it silently. The kids are getting a little antsy. I hand it to Mrs. Abernathy. "You can read it."

Mrs. Abernathy reads part of the letter out loud, then summarizes. "The American Heart Association is donating some of the proceeds from the sale of the stamp to Girasol Zapote's medical treatment and also to further research on the prevention and treatment of Kawasaki disease. And Lincoln Elementary School will be on the news!" She claps again.

Okay, so I'm pretty excited. It's great for Mrs. Abernathy and Lincoln Elementary. It's great for Girasol and my mom and dad. It's great for all the kids who will benefit from the research. But is it great for me? The artist? The one who worked hard on the calendar page so I could win the money? I see my new bike floating on a fluffy cloud, and then—*poof*—it just vaporizes into thin air. I mean, what do *I* get? A plaque. Whippy-skippy. But I know that's not grown-up thinking. Okay, you say it first. Now, let's say it together. *Be the better man, Sandro.*

After class, Mrs. Abernathy tells me that when the school board didn't select my page for the calendar, she decided to submit it for the American Heart Association contest. Wow, Mrs. Abernathy is a great teacher, isn't she? And I've got to give it to Miss Hamilton for actually giving my page to Mrs. Abernathy. Maybe she's not so bad after all.

I swagger out to join my class and crash right into my dad. He's holding his hat in his hands, which are black with tar.

"I missed the ceremony. Congratulations, my son."

I stick out my hand, but he grabs me and hugs me. He whispers in my ear, "We're very proud of you, Sandro."

Then he rubs his dirty hand across his eyes and jams his hat back on his head.

"I love you, Papi!" I shout after him, not even caring that my whole class hears me.

•

Back in class, I keep thinking about winning the stamp contest, and I decide it's cooler than the calendar. People all over the United States will buy the stamp. My name is really, really tiny, but it's there. The calendar pages that Miguel and Abiola designed will be no good next year, but the stamp will be a collector's item forever.

And Mrs. Abernathy said thousands of dollars will be donated to the American Heart Association. Thousands, she said. Two hundred dollars is measly compared to that. I'm sure if I work at it, I can find odd jobs around the neighborhood and save up enough for a new bike by spring.

Miss Hamilton calls up the next reading group, and as Abiola walks by my desk, I see her tilt her head down to sneak a peek at what I'm clicking open and shut.

"I'll show you at recess," I whisper.

"Congratulations on the stamp. It is very cool," she says.

I finish my spelling practice just as Rafe, the messenger for the week, comes by to collect it. We're not really on speaking terms after the Abiola incident, so I'm not surprised when he bumps the pencil off my desk as he grabs my paper. He delivers the papers to Miss Hamilton.

I'm minding my own business, clicking my new gadget, when I hear Miss Hamilton demand, "Sandro. What do you have?"

I quickly jam it in my desk and hold up my hands. "Nothing."

Abiola has that I-swallowed-a-bird look on her face. Well, I'll be. She tattled on me again.

"Sandro. Did you hear me? Will you please come here?" She motions to me with her index finger. I slowly extricate myself from my desk and walk to the back table. Miss Hamilton holds out her hand. "What do you have?"

"Nothing."

"What's in your pocket?"

"Nothing."

"Let's see what nothing looks like, shall we?"

"But Miss Ham . . ." Back me up here. You know I have nothing in my pocket, right? It's in my desk.

She shushes me with her hand. "Did I ask you to talk? Sandro, can't you see that I am trying to teach a reading group? Can't you also see that you are interrupting us? And do you realize that you are wasting our learning time because you are refusing to follow directions?"

The five students at the reading table look pleased as punch to be interrupted, and Abiola's eyes are big as soccer balls. I'm torn. Hold my ground or surrender?

"Sandro? Did you hear me?" Miss Hamilton looks toward the front of the room. "Rafe, did you see Sandro put something in his pocket?"

Rafe? Maybe he saw it when he knocked my pencil off. I knew he was mad at me. While Rafe is squirming, Abiola is waving her arm wildly in the air.

"Abiola, put your hand down," says Miss Hamilton. What else was Abiola going to tell her? That it's not in my pocket but in my desk?

I'm beginning to get upset. First of all, I thought Abiola and I were off to a new start. Second, she has no idea what my new gadget even is. And third, it's none of her business. Anyway, I hear somebody snort a laugh, and out of the corner of my eye, I see Miguel kick the chair in front of him. Rafe's chair. *Yah*, I think. *Don't laugh at a man when he's down.*

Miss Hamilton changes tactics. She stands up and puts her hand on my shoulder and looks me in the eye. "Let's not make this a big deal, shall we? You have a choice, don't you? Do you want to give it to me? Or go see Mr. Smalley?"

"I won't use it anymore. It's nothing, honest."

"Then why won't you give it to me?" Everyone in the class is turned toward the showdown. Miss Hamilton speaks to me slowly and clearly as if I'm deaf or three years old. "Do you know that if you just give me what is in your pocket, you will not be in as much trouble?"

I'm getting steamed. It's only November, and so far she's taken my super ball, my trick hand buzzer, loads of candy, a finger skateboard, and, of course, my calendar page.

"Where did you get it, Sandro?"

"The store."

"What store?"

"The store on the corner, Mr. Chin's."

"And why did you buy it?"

"I thought it was cool."

"Do you know how disappointed your parents will be when Mr. Smalley calls them?"

Yes, I did forget about that. My mom's face, so proud of me this morning, and my dad, taking time off work to come see me. But it's the principle of the thing. Kids have rights, don't they? And the pride of the thing. My pride just won't let me use my good judgment. And to be brutally honest, it's about the power to control my own destiny. I mean, it's just a silly gadget, but it's *mine*. Think about all I've lost in the past month. Bike. Soccer tournament. Recycling money. And almost my sister.

Before you can say jack-in-the-box, my temper takes over. I can't control it. It's a fireball in my chest. This is the last straw. I'm tired of losing. I hear the words exploding from my mouth. "Why don't you just—"

But something stops me. I'm about to say, "—leave me alone, you fat cow." Actually three things stop me.

Abiola stops me. She's shaking her head and giving me the unmistakable sign that means stop while you're ahead. Maybe I confused her I-swallowed-a-bird look with her I-will-run-interference-for-you look.

The thought of my mom stops me. Didn't she just tell me the face of your enemy hides the heart of a friend? Miss Hamilton played a big part in my soon-to-be-famous stamp.

I stop myself. Think about how hurt Miss Hamilton would be if I turned around and started name-calling. I'm the new and improved Sandro, now. Sandro the better man.

"Just a minute. I'll get it." I sheepishly slink back to my desk. Out of the corner of my eye, I see Abiola whisper to Miss Hamilton. What is Abiola doing?

I put my new gadget with its slick bone handle and its silver button on the table. I'm afraid it will be the last time I see it. It's a little greasy from using it. Miss Hamilton picks it up with two fingers and slides it into an envelope. It leaves a little streaked mark on the table. Then she writes out a note.

My heart sinks. I know we're not allowed to bring toys and such to school, but she's never written me a note before. And how is this less trouble than it would have been if I'd refused to hand it over? Here it is, only November, and I'm on a slippery slope. It's going to be a long, long, long year.

I look around. It's as though I've cast a spell on the whole class. Like in *Sleeping Beauty* when even the flies stop buzzing. I'm sure you could hear the eyelash of a gnat fall to the ground.

Miss Hamilton hands me the envelope and the note. "Take this to Mr. Smalley."

I walk out into the hall. This is the story of my life. My office friends are curious when I first walk in, but when they see the note, their faces look dismayed like they can't believe I messed up again. I think Mrs. Lopez even feels sorry for me. And I feel sorry for myself. Like I've let them down, just when they trusted me to turn over a new leaf.

I want to tell them it's still me. Just a little mistake. Actually another little mistake, but don't focus on that. Focus on the *real* me—the new Sandro.

Me, winner of the American Heart Association stamp. Me, philanthropist aluminum can recycler. Me, the master of paper clipping and errand running.

Mrs. Lopez points me to Mr. Smalley's door, and I knock. I hear him say, "Come in." He motions me to my usual chair. It's a very uncomfortable chair. My feet don't reach the floor, and my back can't slouch without the wooden slats pressing into me. He reads the note and gets a funny look on his face.

All because of Abiola and her tattletaling. See if I ever invite her to play soccer again. I guess my mom was wrong when she said sometimes the face of your enemy hides the heart of your friend. Bah. More likely that sometimes the face of your enemy hides the heart of a *fiend*.

Mr. Smalley takes the contraption out of the envelope and pushes the button on the bone handle. *Click.* The black serrated plastic edge pops out. He holds it in front of his eyes, and I can see the light between the teeth of the comb. He tries it a couple more times. I bet he wishes he had one. His hair could use it. Maybe I should tell him about Mr. Chin's. Then he wipes his hands on a tissue.

"Sandro, Miss Hamilton says you can retrieve your toy when school is over. She's concerned because Rafe thought you had a switchblade, and anything that looks like a weapon falls under our No Tolerance policy."

"A switchblade?" My mind is reeling. Number one—I have never even seen a switchblade. I thought the bone handle was a clever way to store a comb. Number two—I would never bring a weapon to school no matter what.

And number three. I realize Rafe got me into trouble. Not Abiola. Rafe? My brain is putting two and two together. No wonder he knocked my pencil on the floor so he could see my gadget. But why did he tell Miss Hamilton I had a switchblade? And what does he know about switchblades, anyway? Why didn't he just ask me what it was? He must still be mad at me or jealous. Maybe that's it. I used to play soccer with him and stand in line with him and talk to him. Lately Miguel and me and Abiola are always together.

Mr. Smalley keeps talking. "Abiola told Miss Hamilton it was only a comb, but to be on the safe side, she wants me to hold on to it. She also says she's very pleased with your new attitude and self-control."

The ball of fire anger in my chest is now a little warm glow. My heart feels pretty big right now. So that's why Abiola was waving her hand and whispering to Miss Hamilton. I move Abiola into my friend lineup in the number two spot right after Miguel. And to think that Miss Hamilton wrote those nice things about me. Well, let's have a great year, Miss Hamilton, shall we? Rafe on the other hand . . . oh, who cares about Rafe? I shouldn't hold it against him, should I? I mean, if he really thought it was a switchblade, holy guacamole. *Be the better man, Sandro.*

Mr. Smalley writes out a hall pass, and I start to leave his office when I see my office fans and their worried looks.

"Mr. Smalley, can I borrow my comb for just a minute?"

I show them how I comb my hair with my cool gadget. My dad's hair gel is really getting a workout today. Then I hand it back to Mr. Smalley. Next time I have ten dollars lying around, I might get him one.

I'm zipping back to class when I round the corner by the staircase, and I remember my very first visit to Mr. Smalley's office. I have an idea. I glance around and head up to the third floor. At the top of the landing,

I take a minute to make a little paper airplane out of my hall pass. I wish it were bigger, but the paper is that smooth kind, so it's easy to fold and has just the right weight to it.

I lean over the railing and launch my creation. It sails down and down and down, spiraling perfectly. Hmmm. Maybe I'll be an aeronautical engineer when I grow up. I race down the stairs two at a time, and when I get to the bottom, guess who's holding my airplane?

"Perhaps, I should just walk you back to class, Sandro," Mr. Smalley says with a wink. "I'm on my way to let teachers know we will be going outside for recess after all, now that the rain's stopped."

My class is lining up in the hall when me and my new pal, princi-pal, that is, walk up. Everybody hears the news and retreats to grab coats. Abiola gives me cuts in line. She's holding her awesome soccer ball. We sprint out the door and across the playground to the soccer field.

"Come on," I yell at Rafe, who I see standing by himself near the building wall. "You can be on our team!"

Acknowledgments

S andro has a village that helps to raise him. Parents who love him. Teachers, coaches, and neighbors who care. Friends who stand by him. It also takes a village to publish a book. My village includes my husband who patiently listens to my first dribbly drafts; my kids and grandkids who fill my life with love (Ashley, Ardell, Brian, Abbie, Kevin, Hazel, and Hank); my writing sisters who challenge and inspire me (Chris DeSmet, Julie Holmes, Blair Hull, Roi Solberg, Cheryl Hansen, and Lisa Kusko); the office staff at Allen School who do the many unseen jobs of making kids feel safe and welcome besides helping me with my

Spanish words; Mrs. Klotz's fifth grade class who read *Canned and Crushed* before it was even published; and, of course, the amazing duo of Julie Matysik, my editor, and Adrienne Szpyrka, her assistant, who will die when they see the length of this paragraph and in the sweetest of ways will help me edit it!

About the Author

....

Hi, I'm Mac. Full name: MacBook Air. Bibi and I started seeing each other when she broke if off with Sam. Samsung Netbook. We've had our conflicts, mainly fighting about backspacing and two-finger tracking, but I'm predicting ours will be a lasting relationship. Bibi hates to talk about herself, so she asked me to write a few words on her behalf.

She graduated from Westmont College in California with a BA in English, then moved to Aurora, Illinois, to begin her teaching career. She's completed Reading Recovery training, an ESL endorsement, a Reading Endorsement, and a master's in Bilingual

Literacy. She's taught first, second, and third grade, Reading Recovery, reading intervention groups, and has also been a literacy coach. As close as I can calculate, she's taught more than one thousand kids to read.

She's a mother of four kids and Grandma Bibi to Hazel and Hank. She writes books she thinks her students will like because she wants to inspire them to be meaning makers and change agents. She loves the beach and sunsets over Lake Michigan but leaves me at home in my neoprene. She loves movies with characters that make positive changes, but she gets greasy popcorn butter all over my keys. She loves reading all kinds of genres almost as much as spending time with me.

We're done here, aren't we? You can always contact me on her webpage for additional information. She and I have no secrets.